SHADOWSELVES

SHADOWSELVES

— Stories —

Jason Ockert

DZANC
BOOKS

DZANC BOOKS

5220 Dexter Ann Arbor Rd.
Ann Arbor, MI 48103
www.dzancbooks.org

Library of Congress Cataloging-in-Publication Data Available Upon Request

ISBN: 978-1-950539-39-0
First US edition: February 2022
Interior design by Michelle Dotter

The following stories have been previously published, some in slightly different form:
"Golden Vulture" in *Granta*; "Five Miles from Home" in *Phantom Drift;* "Your Nearest Exit May be Behind You" in *Shenandoah*; "The Salt Life" in *Juxtaprose;* "The Immortal Jellyfish" in *BULL: Men's Fiction*; "Every Heavy Thing" in *We Can't Help it if We're From Florida: New Stories from a Sinking Peninsula*; "Y'idiot" in *Bridge Eight*; "Mrs. Hutchinson's Bones" in *Cover Stories*; and "Erase the Days" in *The Cincinnati Review*.

Printed in the United States of America

10 9 8 7 6 5 4 3 2 1

Contents

For D, G, and J

GOLDEN VULTURE

THE TURKEY VULTURES GLIDE on updrafts in the lazy blue sky. They circle counter-clockwise, stirring the afternoon. They're dutifully drawn to decaying flesh. The more putrid the carcass, the more pungent the scent, the more birds in the kettle.

By the boy's count, there are eight turkey vultures but he's really only interested in the one with golden wings. It whirls with the others, loop by loop, easy to spot even at a distance.

At first, Hoyt thought it might be a trick of the light. Sunshine in summertime can be deceptive. He's seen diamonds evaporate from blades of grass and quarters shimmering at the bottom of the community pool turn into wads of gum. From his tree fort, he's watched sparks of gold rise from the earth and hover in the branches. Before his childhood brain can right itself, those fireflies are worth a fortune.

Hoyt has given the vulture ample opportunity to prove it doesn't exist. He recently turned ten, which is an in-between age in terms of make-believe. He hasn't lost all his baby teeth but he has lost faith in the Tooth Fairy. When a knocking sound startles him awake in the middle of the night, he knows it's just the wind. His imaginary friends have been replaced by unimaginative flesh-and-blood boys. A teacher once said that when you hear a ringing in your ear it means someone is thinking about you, and although he wishes this was true and that his mother was thinking of him on the few occasions when he's heard a high-pitched tingle, he's not buying it. He doesn't believe in ghosts but he's not ready to dismiss God. Satan seems silly but he has sensed demons.

Sometimes Hoyt feels an entity beside him. It's a warm pulse of energy that suddenly descends for no discernable reason. It only appears when the boy blinks which means he can never see it. The thrumming energy is a version of himself—a *shadow*self—living a heartbeat in the past or else a heartbeat in the future. Sometimes the shadowself is trying to hold him back. Sometimes it tugs him forward. Either way, he has no idea what it wants. He wonders if he is a shadowself to a different blinking Hoyt living in another dimension. Maybe that other Hoyt wonders what the here-and-now Hoyt wants, too.

Hoyt spotted the bird through binoculars from his tree fort in the woods behind his house shortly after he scarfed down a bologna sandwich. It's early June, when the whippoorwills trill and ants stretch the ground into wavering segmented lines. After determining the wings were really gold, Hoyt concocted his plan. He fetched his slingshot, a pillowcase, and some duct tape. Now all he has to do is shoot it down, wrap its beak, carry it home, and cram it into Grainger's dog carrier. The dead dog doesn't need it no more. After that, he'll pull out feathers and grow into a rich, rich man.

The boy begins his adventure tired but in high spirits. He moves quickly with his unusual gait. Hoyt lopes. Always has. Instead of swinging arms, pumping legs, and holding his head high, the boy keeps his spine straight, shoulders hunched, elbows pinned to his side and head down. He takes two-step strides. He's learned to walk this way by treading on every other crosstie between the rails.

There is no train anymore. Hasn't been for as long as the boy remembers. The tracks are a quarter mile behind his modest house in his quiet neighborhood. "Used to not be so quiet," says Dad. Dad works the graveyard shift with the road crew on the interstate and sleeps through the days. Back then, even without the big racket, there was always the anticipation of sound, his father has explained. "I still hear it echoing in my skull. The damned trains woke the dog who woke you and once you started wailing there was no stopping it. The racket drove your mother up a wall. Then out the door."

Hoyt has no memory of being a screaming baby, nor does he recollect when his mother left. The last time he asked his dad why she left, he said, "We already discussed this." That's all he's ever said, as far back as Hoyt can remember, so now the boy is convinced they must have discussed it even though he has no memory of that discussion and cannot, for the life of him, pinpoint the reason for the leaving. Maybe the discussion happened when he was rapidly blinking and his father confused him for his shadowself. If the shadowself knows the reason Mom disappeared, Hoyt hopes he'll figure out a way to share it with him soon.

The only evidence of a train and a mother is a photograph Hoyt keeps in his sock drawer. In the shot, his five-year-old self is hoisting an ice cream sundae so big it covers the lower half of his face. His mother has a cherry perched between her lips and she is laughing. Laughing, Hoyt guesses, at something funny Mr. Loco just said.

Back when there were trains, there was an ice cream boxcar called *Locomotive's*. The owner referred to himself as Mr. Loco. He wore a multicolored conductor's hat and handed out complimentary plastic toy whistle cabooses. When the train ground to a halt, he'd throw open a window, crank up his catchy ditty—"Go *Cra*-zy for Ice Cream 'cuz Ice Cream's *Cra*-zy for you!"—and the wide-eyed kids who lived along the tracks would scuttle out of their ramshackle houses with their sweat-stained clothes and ill-fitting shoes and gobble up everything offered. Once the passengers were all aboard, Mr.

Loco was off to the next stop. The sticky-mouthed children slouched back to where they were from.

The few stories Dad has told about Mom always feature her sad. Down, out, fidgety. Couldn't keep her hands still, he said. In the picture, though, she seems as happy as anyone Hoyt has seen. She's purposefully crossing her eyes. Clowning around. Her thin wrists are turned upward, hands bent at odd angles frozen in some goofy dance. There's a strand of her hair dipping into Hoyt's hot fudge.

You can't see Mr. Loco in the photograph, but the boy knows he's there because of one hairy hand hovering near Mom's neck. Against her alabaster skin his sharp fingernails are dirty and long. In the shot, Mr. Loco appears to be reaching for Mom's throat.

That picture was taken a half-lifetime ago. Shortly after, Mom left and the trains quit.

———

Railroad weeds slope up the embankment and shoot out of the gravelly soil between the ties. The track resembles the exposed spine of a dormant rust dragon waiting to awaken and rise from the earth. The boy used to hope he'd be there when the dragon awoke so he could clutch its neck and flap off to some remote, rusty island. He'd have his cool pet smite anyone that got in his way. Then Hoyt felt guilty for imagining a better pet while Grainger, with his hip dysplasia and incontinence, still wagged his patchy tail and cast half-lidded, rheumy, optimistic eyes up at the boy every time Hoyt hurried outside.

So, no dragons. No pets. The golden-winged turkey vulture is a business acquisition. To maintain a sense of distance from it, he's not even going to give it a name. Leprechauns and genies are never given names, after all. Wishers don't want to get too emotional with their prize-givers or else they'll start feeling rotten about their wishes.

Just because there aren't trains doesn't mean there isn't danger along the rail. Hoyt's allowed to traipse as far north as the water tower and south to Miller's Gorge. Under no circumstance is he allowed onto the railway bridge. Last summer, while father and son were doing dishes in the kitchen and watching the sun set, Dad gave two reasons why Hoyt was forbidden to cross that bridge. Dad, in fact, often gives two reasons. He has offered two reasons why you shouldn't leave the front door open (you let the air conditioning escape and flies come in). There are two reasons you make your bed every morning (to keep your room presentable in case of a visitor and because it's better to fall asleep when the sheets are tight). If he can't think of a mate for a single reason he'll say, "And also, because I said so."

The first reason Dad offered for not crossing the bridge is that Hoyt might slip and fall to his death in the rocky ravine below. A half-dozen folks a year die this way. (And though Dad didn't mention it, Hoyt's heard the rumors that some sad people hang themselves from a faded red plank on the trestle.) The second reason Dad gave is that Burch is bad news.

Burch used to be a coal-producing company town that had a school, library, bowling alley, shopping mall, and a roller-skating rink. Then many of the miners got black lung and sued the company before dying. The lawyers made a killing. The company went belly up. Now Burch is Burch in name only. Those who could afford to scurry away did. Everyone else stayed and waited for a coalman with a conscience to roll into town and make the mines operational and safe. "Fat chance of that," Dad said, drying a milk glass with a dish towel. "Only a fool believes in miracles. What's worse is when a fool quits believing. Then he becomes desperate. And desperate folks," Dad said, dropping a moist hand on his boy's shoulder, "are dangerous. So stay out of Burch."

———

Last summer, the boy still believed in miracles. That's why he disobeyed his father and crossed the bridge. He wondered, back then, if his mother might be over there. (He did not wonder, for long, if his mother noosed her neck and did the flop, twitch, and dangle over the ravine hitched to the suicide tie.)

For one full week Hoyt loped over to Burch and searched for her. He started out with high hopes. One time Grainger had run away and the boy found him limping along a fence line near Shotts' farm. The dog had been bitten by some kind of venomous snake—maybe a rattler. Grainger survived the ordeal but was never really the same afterward. Last summer Hoyt hoped he'd find his mother, too, with or without a snakebite. If need be, the boy would carry her back in his arms the same way he did with Grainger. In Burch, Hoyt visited the few remaining shops in the ruined mall. He went to the barber shop. He loitered outside three different bars, places where he felt sorrow ooze out every time the front door opened. At the end of that week last summer, Hoyt had learned three things:

1. Neither crossing a railway bridge nor the ruined town of Burch was really dangerous.

2. Mom wasn't there.

3. Miracles schmiracles.

If he knew, Dad would say hunting a golden-winged turkey vulture is dumb and dangerous. But Dad doesn't know. He's slumbering at home and won't wake for hours.

Ordinarily Hoyt doesn't hear his Dad return around four. This morning, his father slammed the front door and startled the boy awake. He wasn't able to fall back asleep. Eating breakfast at the kitchen counter, Hoyt decided he was going to take a nap in the treehouse later. That was before he saw the golden-winged bird. There's no time for napping now. The day is bright. Summer break yawns across the calendar.

The boy carries the pillowcase over his shoulder, Santa Claus style. Inside with the duct tape are a dozen donut-hole-sized rocks he's gathered from the creek bed. The frame of the slingshot is made of steel with surgical tubing attached to the uprights. The pocket is made of genuine leather. Closing one eye, slowing his breathing, and drawing the sling back to the tip of his nose, Hoyt can smash a bottle from twenty yards away, easy. The weapon was a recent birthday gift from his grandfather—his mother's father—who sent it all the way from Alaska. After the photo of his mom, the slingshot is his most prized possession.

As he lopes, the boy alternates between checking the sky to make sure the vulture is still circling and looking down to keep from tripping. Soon he's at the bridge, then upon it. The water below is brown. The faded red tie is about midway, and Hoyt steps over it. The clouds are too high and strung out to resemble anything. The warm wind blows through the ravine and it does not cool the boy. Soon, he's across.

On the other side, in Burch, he approaches the dozen or so company homes built nearly atop the tracks. The houses here are tall and thin and resemble half-gallon cartons of chocolate milk stacked side by side. In the heyday, workers would sit on their tiny back porches eating ice cream cones as they waited for the coal train. The men who used to live here were not miners. Their job was to haul the trucks from the mines to the tracks and load the coal into the cars. In between they just had to wait. Last summer Hoyt knocked on every door and inquired about his mom. Nobody knew anything. Hoyt has learned that nobody ever knows anything, really. Not about his mom, not about where all the trains went, not about coal in lungs and death to dogs. The best part of knowing nobody knows anything is that you don't have to feel bad when you don't know something either. Like why some vultures are made out of gold.

Beyond the dilapidated homes is a three-story apartment building. It's a place Hoyt never bothered to visit. Each unit has a small balcony enclosed by a metal rail and the façade reminds him of a set of teeth with braces in bad need of a good brushing. Plastic bags and Styrofoam food cartons litter the unkempt, balding hedges a landscaper once planted in a half-hearted effort to provide privacy from the railroad. In the bright sunlight the imperfections are glaring. Hoyt has to squint to see clearly. Overhead, in the tangle of scavengers, the bird with golden wings soars above the rooftop.

Clinging to the side of the building is a fire escape zigzagging to the third floor. Though the boy could easily climb two steps at once, he crouches low and slinks. Just because the birds are attracted to death doesn't mean they don't fear it. He may only get one shot at this. If his aim is true, his life will change forever. His father can quit work and they can build a fortress. He'll teach Dad how to play video games. They'll horse around in the pool with the waterslide and eat ice cream from bowls made out of cookies. He'll buy a bright blue train and hire someone to paint all of the railroad ties a rainbow pattern and he'll sit in the caboose and throw candy to the awe-stricken children lining the tracks and cotton candy will puff out of the steam pipe and make the air taste sweet.

When the boy's halfway up the rickety staircase, he catches a thick whiff of rot. With every step, the stench grows, and by the time he's at the top he's worn out and his unblinking eyes are wide. The neck of the pillowcase is wet with sweat where he clutches it. There, on the stained concrete balcony floor, is a large, oval-shaped platter heaped with a pile of dead rats. Bright white teeth gleam in the sunlight. The long, slender tails drape over the lip of the plate. When the hovering pulse of black flies lands upon the mess, wiry whiskers quiver.

A sudden shift in the breeze blows the putrid scent full over the boy and he turns his entire body away to shield himself. He staves off a rising gag and dips his mouth and nose into his shirtfront.

Then Hoyt hears someone say, "Hello?" and he realizes he's not alone. There's a partially open sliding glass door that leads from the balcony into the apartment. Against the glare of the glass, it's impossible for him to see inside. What he can see is his reflection and he's embarrassed by it. Here is a cowering boy with his face tucked into his sweat-drenched shirt a heartbeat away from fleeing. That's not how he imagined he'd look when he started out on this adventure. Before he has time to remake himself, the glass door slides fully open and in its place is a thin woman in a hooded sweatshirt and loose jeans. Her dark hair is shocked in streaks of gray and it shoots out from her head in a wild revolt. The woman's face is aggravated by red splotches as if she were mindlessly rubbing fingertips against her forehead, temples, and jaw. Her eyes are all pupils, two black holes sucking in cavernous cheekbones. When she opens her mouth to speak, her dry lips reluctantly unseal.

"I was expecting you around front," she says.

Hoyt slides his shirt down so the woman can see his face clearly. He wants to show her he isn't who she thinks he is.

The woman's expression doesn't change. "Come on in," she says before disappearing inside.

If Dad were here, he'd have more than two reasons why Hoyt shouldn't follow the woman into the apartment. Surely it's a trap. She probably poisoned the rats in order to poison the golden-winged vulture. A woman like that might try to poison him, too. It was foolish of the boy to think he was the only one who had spotted it. Of course she would expect company. For all he knows, more prospectors are on their way. He'll have to proceed with caution.

It takes a few moments to blink out the daylight so Hoyt's eyes

can adjust to the darkness inside. The space is small. There's a wood-
en coffee table in front of a sagging couch. On the table are a pack
of cigarettes, a lighter, and an ashtray. A rocking chair is positioned
across from the couch. In the tiny dining room, beneath a crooked
light dangling from a brass chain, is an enormous harp. A stool sits
beside it. The harpist, Hoyt presumes, stands at the kitchen counter,
watching him.

"Close the slider," she says. "I can't afford to air condition the
outside."

As far as Hoyt can tell, they are alone. The glass door slides
smoothly shut.

"What took you so long?" the woman asks.

Hoyt sets his pillowcase on the table and stands next to it. In
one fluid motion the boy could brandish the slingshot and defend
himself if things go sideways. "I came as soon as I could."

"You're pretty young to be a runner."

"I'm plenty old," Hoyt says, standing as tall as he can, "and I
didn't run."

"All right," the harpist says. "I'm no one to judge. You are per-
spiring."

"It's hot."

"I'll get you water. Feel free to sit down."

Hoyt shifts his weight onto his heels and crosses his arms. One
thing he's learned from school is that you shouldn't do what a teacher
tells you to do right away or else she'll think she can bully you into
taking tests and doing homework. If he sits when she says sit, he's her
pet. He'll sit if and when it pleases him. Stealing a quick peek outside, he finds the birds are still overhead. "I guess your plan is poison.
That's not what I had in mind."

The harpist turns the faucet on and murky water pours into a
green coffee mug. "What?"

"I was just going to stun it and pluck feathers one by one as needed. If you kill it, you cut off the supply."

Turning the faucet off, the harpist holds the mug in her hand and frowns. "I'm not following you."

"The golden-winged vulture. Outside." The boy juts his chin at the slider.

The harpist isn't wearing shoes. Hoyt notices this as she crosses from the kitchen tile onto the stained carpet in the living room to stand by his side. "There's somebody out there? Were you followed?"

"No," Hoyt says, his voice cracking. "I'm talking about the golden-winged vulture."

"The what? Golden vulture?"

"Up there. With the others," Hoyt points.

The harpist follows the boy's finger. Her thin face remains puzzled. "Yeah, I see them. They're the signal."

"What signal?"

"The signal that notifies Mr. Loco. Tells him I'm ready for a delivery. Those are his rules, not mine. I didn't order Golden Vulture."

"Who did you just say?"

"Mr. Loco," the harpist replies. Barefoot, she's two inches taller than the boy. "You do work for him, right?"

Hoyt keeps his mouth shut and tries to work through the confusion. Either the woman has terrible breath or else he can smell the rot from the rats outside seeping in through the slider. The apartment seems to be getting cloudy. There's a vein as small as a thread twitching against the papery skin beneath the harpist's right eye.

"So you don't work for him?"

"No."

"You saw the birds and came on your own?"

"I came for the golden vulture. You and I can work out a deal, but I'm not sharing with anyone else."

The two stand in silence, studying one another. The boy wants to ask about Mr. Loco so badly he can't bring himself to do so. The man might know where his mother is. Hoyt had no idea Mr. Loco was still in business and that he delivered his ice cream. Of course, it makes sense. People might not need coal anymore but they still need dessert.

"I think I will sit down," Hoyt says. He slumps onto the couch and places his hands in his lap.

The harpist, still clutching the mug of water, shifts her dark eyes from the boy to the bag on the coffee table. "Golden Vulture?" she repeats.

"Yeah. I guess Mr. Loco knows about it."

"If he does, he didn't mention it to me."

"Well, it's here now."

"I see," the harpist says, folding her arms. She holds the coffee mug crooked. A trickle of water spills onto her sleeve. "What does Golden Vulture do?"

"It changes our lives."

"How much does it cost?"

"It doesn't cost anything. It pays *us* if we can get it."

"I see," the harpist says again, and when she says this Hoyt knows she actually doesn't see. People only repeat themselves when they're uncertain. He can tell the harpist is scheming. Her eyebrows are bunched together, her lips are slanted into a false smile, and she is breathing out of her mouth. This is exactly the same expression the boy adopts when he's scheming.

If his mind wasn't so full he might be able to draw the comparison by glancing at his reflection in the sliding glass door. Neither boy nor harpist notices the similarities. In both heads wheels turn. Gears grind.

Hoyt's old plan was to capture the vulture and live like a king. Actually, the *old* old plan—the reason he visited Burch last year—was to track down his mom. Though Hoyt doesn't believe in fate, it is a strange coincidence that the golden-winged vulture led him to the harpist who ordered ice cream from Mr. Loco who used to know his mother. That's a fact. The proof is in the photograph.

"You know," the harpist says, "I might have some doughnuts in the pantry. Do you like doughnuts?"

"What kind?"

"Glazed."

"Glazed are my favorite."

The harpist returns to the kitchen. She pulls a box of doughnuts from the pantry and arranges them on a plate. "I'm going to make you some lemonade," she says. For a moment she disappears beneath the sink. When she stands back up, she pours a white powder out of a Tupperware container into the mug. Withdrawing a teaspoon, she stirs the drink slowly. Then she gathers the items and moves into the living room. She sets the plate on the coffee table and the mug and spoon beside the lighter. Up close the boy can see that her fingernails are ragged, bitten down to jagged and inflamed slivers. Her hands are trembling as if she is trying to control a rising fear or else escalating excitement. "Help yourself."

Probably, the boy decides, the food isn't poisoned. He just saw her take the doughnuts out of the pantry. Besides, the harpist isn't threatening. Also, he's suddenly ravenous. Lunch was eons ago. He snatches a doughnut, takes a big bite, and chews with his mouth open—a habit his father has failed to break. "Do you play?" the boy mumbles.

"Not well anymore."

A familiar faraway sadness creeps into the harpist's wet eyes. He says, "I'm sure that's not true. I bet you're real good."

"I used to be decent. I was in an orchestra."

"Why'd you quit?"

"I didn't. I was cut."

"How come?"

"I slipped on a patch of ice and snapped my wrist. Just like that, my dreams ended. The bone healed funny. Look," she says, holding up her arm. "See how crooked?"

"Yeah."

"A weak wrist means slow fingers. If your fingers don't fly, the harp will chomp you up."

Hoyt swallows down the last of the doughnut. He considers the instrument and says, "It looks like a mouth. I've never seen one in person before."

"Some say it resembles a wing."

"I can see that."

"Have you ever heard it?"

"I don't think so."

"You have, you just don't remember. Here. I'll play you something." She enters the dining room, adjusts the stool, straddles the short end of the instrument, and tilts the body of the harp toward her. Her head is on the other side of the strings, and it appears as if she is looking at the boy through bars. Or else the other way around: the boy is the one in the cage.

"This is called glissando," she says, draping her arms around the harp and quickly running her thumbs and fingertips from one end to the other.

Hoyt snags a second doughnut from the plate and reclines into the couch so he has a better view. "Cool."

"I'll play a little bit of *Fantasia*. You'll recognize the tune. It's about a sorcerer's apprentice."

The harpist gently plucks the strings and coaxes out a rhythm. Her body sways while her face remains tight and severe. Her eyes stay locked on Hoyt. Whatever sadness they held is gone. When she speaks the boy cannot see her lips move. Her words rise out of the harp.

"Be sure to wash that down with lemonade."

Hoyt lifts the mug to his lips. In the dim, bluish afternoon light the liquid looks brown. When he takes a sip, it tastes bitter. "Are you sure this isn't tea?"

"Tell me about Golden Vulture," the harpist says. "How does it make you feel?"

"Excited, of course."

"Euphoric?"

"Maybe. I don't know what that means."

"Real good."

"I think I'll feel real good if I can catch it." Hoyt gulps the lemonade to see if it tastes more like lemonade the second time around. It doesn't so he drinks more. Then he decides it's tea, which he doesn't like. He picks another doughnut from the plate.

"Do you recognize the score?"

"The what?"

"The melody."

"Not really."

"Try a little harder."

Hoyt devours the doughnut and listens. Eventually, he says, "Maybe I have heard it. My mom might have played it when I was younger." Hoyt sinks further into the couch and props his head on the arm. "She knows Mr. Loco," Hoyt says. "He made her laugh."

"He makes many mothers happy."

"Do you think he'll be here soon?"

"Close your eyes. Picture the apprentice dressed in his red robes. See him wave his hands. He believes he's in charge of the entire universe. He conducts lightning and thunder. He sends the waves high into the sky." The harpist moves her fingers like nimble spiders; the song sounds like it's having a panic attack.

Hoyt takes one last big bite and then closes his eyes. "I remember. He wore a purple hat, didn't he? With stars on it."

"But he was only dreaming," she says quietly. "No matter how badly he yearns to be a magician, he's only the apprentice."

Hoyt listens. A gathering blanket of darkness presses down.

After some time has passed, the harpist says, "Can I ask you something?"

"Sure," the boy says. The music has stopped, he thinks. Maybe he can still hear it.

"What are you going to do with your fingers?"

"What?"

"Your fingers. They're sticky. From the doughnuts. Why don't you lick them clean?"

"All right," the boy says, though he doesn't move.

"Maybe," the harpist says, "you won't mind if I have a taste."

The boy's not certain he heard right. He thinks she's asking him to leave her the last doughnut. That is, if there is another doughnut left. He can't remember if he ate them all. It's too much work to open his eyes and check. "That's fine," he says.

In the dream, the boy's fingers are cheese. Rats gnaw them down to bone. A wolf knocks, a cauldron bubbles, the hands of a clock stab out his eyes.

———

Hoyt awakens into crimson light. He surveys the room and very little of what he sees makes sense. His empty pillowcase is crumpled on the floor with its contents—the round rocks he gathered from the creek bed and the unused duct tape—strewn across the coffee table. There's a steak knife next to his ruined slingshot. The harpist has severed the surgical tubing. The teaspoon holds a charred black oval. A small glass vial sits next to a plastic red cap. The plate is empty. The rot-stench is more pungent than it was before. The boy's fingertips are red and raw. The harpist slumps in the rocking chair, a syringe at her bare feet. Her sweatshirt sleeves are rolled up. The tubing from his slingshot is draped around her left arm. Her eyes are cast in the general direction of the boy. There's blood on her lips and a thorn in her smile.

"You poisoned me," Hoyt mutters. "You ruined my slingshot." When he sits up, his dizzy body seems to follow a heartbeat behind. "I missed Mr. Loco." A part of him longs for sleep. A darker part is breaking free.

His shadowself accelerates. Without warning, Hoyt snaps. In a blink, he's off the couch, snatching the knife, and with quick, methodical precision he jabs the blade deeply into the harpist's chest. The wet sucking sound each slash makes is punctuated by a warm blood spray. The sensation feels familiar. It rings a bell. He's done all this before. The reason his mother is gone is because he killed her. Stab, stab, stab, stab, stab.

After a while, the whir stills. The boy's body catches up with the boy. Reason returns. Mom's not dead, she's just gone. The shadow scuttles back into the folds of his brain.

Hoyt sits on the couch with his upturned hands on his knees. He's sweating and breathing heavy. The harpist is in the chair making choking noises. She not dead or dying. She's laughing.

"What's so funny?"

"I couldn't figure out why you came. But I see now." The harpist has turned her wobbly eyes toward the balcony. "That gold bird. It's all yellow pain," she says, before doubling over in laughter and nearly tumbling out of the rocker.

"Pain?"

"Yellow pain," she spits out.

On the balcony, the golden-winged vulture is fretting over the rats. Up close, Hoyt can see that its reddish head is the same color as the suicide tie. The hooked beak dips and rends. Its unblinking gray-brown eyes nest in a wrinkled face. The tops of the wings are black. Only the underside—which Hoyt glimpses when the bird flaps its wings to ward away the other vultures—is golden. Although, it's not gold. It's yellow paint.

He locates a truth in the vulture's eyes: a scavenger, descending upon carrion along the side of a freshly painted Interstate. With the vulture perched so close, it's easy for Hoyt to imagine its rapturous feasting. He can picture it flailing its wings in order to claim its portion of the kill. He can envision it along the highway shoulder, sloshing in wet paint and slick blood, gorging with abandon while cars whiz close and swiftly by. And now it's here eating poisoned rats with single-minded hunger. The boy can't decide if before him is a stupid beast or a fearless survivor.

Hoyt stands and collects his things. He opens the slider and the vultures scatter. He steps over the remains of the rats, descends the stairs, and leaves the sorceress in her hysterical delirium. Outside, it's darker than Hoyt expects, later than he realized. He walks toward the tracks and, through the dwindling twilight, heads home. His mother is and isn't in Burch. Hoyt suspects that he is not alone with his shadowself. There may be a vast army of shadowselves shoving and tugging at other people as they blink through their days.

When he's upon the railway bridge, Hoyt observes a flock of thrushes rising out of the ravine into the cooling air to hunt mosquitoes. Not vultures, not gold. Just birds. It occurs to Hoyt that there are either too many mysteries for the world to possibly contain or else none at all.

FIVE MILES FROM HOME

LAST NIGHT THE BLIZZARD snuffed out the power. It's quiet in the small town tucked between the thumb and forefinger of the Finger Lakes. Roofs are capped with mushroom-shaped mounds of snow; inside, citizens wrap themselves in quilts awaiting light and heat.

Bryce Stadler has been plowing since daybreak. He's cleared a path for the power company to reach the generators.

It's evening now. Not that now looks much different from this morning. Tonight will merely be a shade darker. Gunmetal gray clouds sag so close to the shimmering white, snow-swept earth, they rest on your head. In your head too, if you let them.

Bryce drives a diesel-fueled Ford F-650 truck with a ten-foot Fisher plow mounted to the front frame. Lowered, the blade is Orion's shield. The bite of steel slices a thin layer of asphalt, which peppers the hills Bryce creates in his wake. The neatly compacted piles are the inverse of the night sky: bits of black pavement against a universe of white.

Once it's cleared, the snow-blanketed rural county road Bryce has turned down—the last stretch before he's home—will let people escape from their homes if they want. Not that there's anywhere to go. There's no rush to finish. The road's not going anywhere.

The few houses here are only on one side of the street. The other side is a cornfield, although you wouldn't know that now. The snow renders it a flat, empty space hemmed in by a thick line of trees along the darkening horizon.

Bryce drives distracted. He's tired and half-hypnotized by the splatter and thunk of snow on windshield—here then gone, here then gone, here then gone. His grip on the steering wheel is tight and his jaw is clenched. Hours crammed in the seat have knotted his shoulders and cramped his calf muscles. The vent blows heat thinly from the dust-lined louvers. His skin is cracked and dry. He's got an old bandage on his index finger which is ready to peel off. Last night he was dicing onions for a chili. Once a week he'll make a pot of it which will feed him for three nights. Bryce was chopping away, not paying attention, when he felt the smooth nip from the serrated blade. The cut was deep enough to bleed for twenty-five minutes, and when he finally staunched it he could see a wide gash. He was tempted to tear off the flap of ripped skin but worried it might start bleeding again. Instead, he wrapped it tight in gauze and slapped on a Band-Aid. He rinsed off the mucky onions and tossed them in the chili.

It'll be a cold bowl for dinner.

No power tonight means no television. Like his neighbors, Bryce has a satellite dish bolted to the roof of his house. It's angled toward the ceiling of sky, a cyclops eye frozen and buried. He can't recall what he was going to watch tonight. He only vaguely remembers what he watched last night. Ordinarily, Bryce takes his dinner on the recliner with his TV tray beside him collecting bottles of Molson until he drifts into his technicolor dreams.

He'll have to find something else to do tonight. Maybe thumb through one of the hunting magazines piled in a crooked stack by his nightstand. His uncle keeps bringing them because Bryce keeps promising he's going to read them. It's been a while since he went hunting with his uncle.

One time, in the woods of his boyhood, in the summer, behind his uncle's farm, Bryce was following deer tracks and got turned around. He carried a little recurve bow he'd received for his twelfth birthday and a quiver of wooden arrows. He wandered into a grove of dense elm, and the heavy musk aroma of moss on tree bark intoxicated him. It was how his grandfather's basement smelled. Distracted, he nearly stumbled into the small pond. He'd explored the woods a hundred times and never once discovered a waterhole. Yet, here one was, which meant he was lost.

In his memory it was twilight but it might have been earlier. His eyes followed a spine of crimson sunlight across the water to the bank on the opposite side. There, draped across a low bough, was fishing line at the end of which dangled a bluegill. The cane pole leaned against the trunk. The fish was either dead or it was not. At that distance he couldn't be certain. It moved on its own accord or else swayed because of a breeze. It's difficult to remember wind. Everything was still but for the smallest gyrations from the doomed fish.

Bryce isn't yanked back into reality because he feels the thump. What startles him is the sudden splatter of red on the windshield. It's a fist-sized hunk of furred flesh. The blades sluice it back and forth in a disembodied wave.

Bryce slows and then stops. He shifts to park and clicks the wipers off. Craning his neck, he peers out the back window. The pavement stretches behind him. Through the sprinkling snow and the steely dusk, he can't see far. Opening the door, he puts a boot to the ground and leans half out to get a better look. The ridge of snow is neat and unbroken except for one spot where something juts into the road. At this distance Bryce can't tell what he's clipped. Could be a deer. Could be a pet.

Cinching his heavy coat together at the neck, he climbs out of the truck. Wind needles his face. His deep-set eyes tear and he rapidly tries to blink it away. The patch of flesh is bunched against the defrosted glass. A trickle of sinew clings to the windshield in a jagged, tacky line.

The summer he discovered the pond in the woods, Bryce decided he was going to unhook the bluegill and set it free. He wondered what kind of man would just leave it to dangle.

Using his bow as a walking stick, Bryce carefully scooted around the perimeter of the pond. Bryce's wavering reflection followed a pace behind as he carefully picked his way along the muddy shore. In the shallows, impatient tadpoles squirmed toward land.

Now, he has to watch his step. The plow can't get everything. No road is really even. There are places where water freezes in the pitch. Pockets of black ice can send a ten-ton truck into the ditch or drop a grown man on his ass. What makes it so dangerous is that it's invisible. You only know you're upon it when you've lost control.

The wall of compacted snow is as high as Bryce's shoulder. Gusts of wind infiltrate his ears and carve a tunnel through his head. He can feel a mounting pressure behind his eyes. He's got ratty gloves deep in his coat pocket. These are his backup pair. They're a little better than nothing. His heavy-duty rabbit-fur-lined mittens are in the glovebox.

Bryce stops next to the tip of a mailbox pole jutting out from the mound. He leans against it for support. Then he slides the beige-colored gloves over his frigid hands, careful not to yank the bandage off his pointer finger. Curious to know where he is, Bryce wipes away snow from the mailbox. The house number is 159. The name, *Hoo er*, is affixed to the side of the box in reflective gold stickers. The missing letter could be a p. Maybe a v. Perhaps a k. No matter what letter he tries to insert, the name doesn't ring a bell.

When he'd made his way around the pond to the bluegill, Bryce set his bow down by a well-worn stump. The fishing pole was just a stick with line. He tried, by twirling the tip around and around, to reel the fish to him, but this only created a tangled rat's nest. Setting the pole aside, he reached for the low branch. The tree was strong and young, the wood green and tough, as Bryce recalls. The unyielding branch caused the fish to dip into a divot of mud. Cursing, Bryce placed one foot into the shallows and, holding onto the branch for balance, his reaching fingers gripped the line. Hand over hand he pulled the fish to him. Through the muck the scales glistened. The fish was as long as a hunting blade, and holding it aloft Bryce could see the gills were still. The eyes were cloudy in pockets where they'd dried. The boy was certain it was dead. What he didn't know was if it could come back to life.

The red mess is only a few yards from the mailbox. Bryce fights the wind and steps closer. The blood has frozen bright. Or maybe it only appears that way against the white of the snow. The animal is iced stiff. Its exposed bones look brittle in the cold. The blade has shorn it in two. A fractured spine sticks out like a long, accusing finger. Bryce can't tell if he's looking at the back half or the front. From the size and shape of the carcass, Bryce can tell it's a large dog. The fur is the sable color he's seen on German Shepherds. It likely snuck outside yesterday, got turned around, and froze to death last night. The snow has been burying it all day. The other half might be compacted in the plow.

Bryce's uncle had dogs. They were half wild and mangy, and if they had names, Bryce never knew them. One particular mutt frightened Bryce as a boy. That beast had different-colored eyes—one brown, one gray—and patchy beige fur. Though his uncle said it was harmless, the dog had a way of appearing out of nowhere with its pink gums curled, exposed yellow teeth gleaming, ears flat back, emitting a low snarl of warning. It always seemed a heartbeat from pouncing.

That summer day, Bryce wasn't fearful of his uncle's dogs because he had his bow to protect him. He concentrated on the task of releasing the bluegill. After he'd unhooked it, Bryce stooped low and placed it gently in the water. Then he pinched his eyes shut and said a little prayer because that's what his uncle told him to do whenever you killed an animal, and although it wasn't Bryce who'd killed the bluegill and what he was praying was for it to come back to life, the boy still said a few words to God. It's impossible for Bryce to recollect the exact words he chose. Before he had a chance to open his eyes, he felt a rough hand wrap around his mouth and the heavy weight of a stranger pinning his arms behind his back.

Except for the ones Bryce is creating, there are no footsteps in the snow leading to the house. Although he's tempted to simply climb back into his truck, head home, and sleep for a month, he feels compelled to notify the homeowners about their dog. It's not easy to deliver bad news, but it's the right thing to do.

Snow has drifted to the front door. It is greedy to get inside. Bryce sees the outline of a mat—presumably with the word *Welcome* on it—buried at his feet. An icicle the size of a rhino tusk is poised above a diamond-shaped window next to the door. His reflection is frosted. His skullcap sits crooked on his head. He's got bags under his eyes.

Bryce rings the doorbell, which doesn't work because the power is out. He'd forgotten. So he knocks. Raps his gloved knuckles on the door four times and follows it with a loud "Hello?" Then he waits in silence. He doesn't hear any dogs barking, which could be a good thing or else it could be a bad thing. Bad if there should be a dog responding to the loud pounding. Good if there never was one.

"Hello?" he says again. "Anyone home?" In the alcove of the

front porch, his words echo back. For the briefest instant Bryce is startled by his own voice.

"Yes?"

Bryce hears a faint voice from behind the door. It sounds like a woman or else a child. "Hi," he says. "Sorry to disturb you."

When the person on the other side of the door doesn't respond, Bryce waits. The door is peephole-less. His breath hovers in front of his eyes. "Um," he says, "is Mr. or Mrs. Hoover home?"

Although there isn't a reply, Bryce can sense there's someone on the other side. Humans give off a radiating pulse houses can't contain.

"I know you're there," Bryce says. "I don't mean any harm. I just wanted to know if you have—I mean *had*—a German Shepherd. That's why I'm here. I'm afraid it's dead."

Bryce shifts his weight from boot to boot. He's never been a very good communicator. His former girlfriend complained that he never really said what he meant or meant what he said. *Dodgy*, was the word she used. He worries how his words are being received by Ms. Hoo er now. "I didn't do it," he says. "I mean, he was already dead. Or she. The dog."

"I don't have a dog. Thank you. Please go."

"Do you know which of your neighbors might have had one?"

"No. Please leave or I'll call the police."

Bryce sighs heavy. He knows the phone lines are down. Even if she could get ahold of someone on her cellphone, they'd have a hell of a time negotiating the icy roads. And for what? The last thing he wants to be is a bother. "All right," he says, turning. "I'm going." He picks his way back to the street in the footprints he's made.

What Bryce remembers from the incident that summer is murky. The man's hand smelled like nightcrawlers. When he opened his eyes, the boy saw stars which were, he knows from the remove of years, a trick of the evening light upon the prickly skin of the pond. The fisherman dunked his head under the water. There was kicking and flailing. Choking. All the primitive kid juices flowing. Somehow a pinch of skin slipped between his front teeth. The boy bit to blood. When his attacker let go, Bryce wiggled away. He doesn't remember anything about fleeing. Can't recall the space between the pond and standing numb on a stranger's porch shivering and mute. Can't recall how long he stayed silent or what kind of punishment he received for wandering so far away without telling anyone and for losing his bow. Can't recall whether that bluegill was floating belly up or if it miraculously darted into the depths.

Back by the mailbox, Bryce tries to decide what to do. His truck is idling patiently, waiting to bully the rest of the snow off the road. Exhaust ghosts from the tailpipe and wavers before rising to the cloudbank. There are only a dozen paces between Bryce and the cab. He's only five miles from home.

Shoving his hands deep inside his coat pockets, Bryce turns back to the animal. The jutting spine is crooked. The biting wind sweeping across the field scalps a layer of snow and scatters it like a shaman dusting the dead. In a few hours, the road will be covered again. The dog will disappear, too. It might be weeks before anyone discovers it. For the pet owner, that's too long.

He'll just try one more house. He shakes away the cold and begins the long walk along the plowed road to the neighbor's.

Now that he thinks about it, the summer Bryce got turned around when he was out in the woods behind his uncle's farm he was a man, not a boy. He was turned around, not lost. It was not so long ago, after all. He'd gone out for a walk. To clear his head. He recognized a grove of elm. The basement-musk of bark. Summer light; dappled leaves. A distant woodpecker. Then he heard substantial shuffling. Maybe a deer foraging?

It was no deer. There was a boy. By a pond. With a cane-pole fishing rod. He'd caught a fish. The line was snagged in a branch and the fish dangled a few feet from the surface of the water and out of reach. The wet scales glistened in the afternoon sunlight. Bryce crouched behind a bush to watch the boy, unmolested, in his childhood predicament.

It was an easy problem to solve. Just snap the branch, reel the fish in, unhook it and place it back in the water. Every fisherman knows this. The kid leaned the pole against the trunk of the tree and stared up at the twitching fish. Clearly, it was suffering. Suffocating in the humid air. Though he couldn't see the gill slits from his hiding spot, Bryce knew they were red and heaving. Still, the boy stood.

All the kid had to do was snap the thin branch. Gather the line by hand. Unhook the fish. Place it in the water.

Distracted by these thoughts, Bryce is confused when he approaches the house next to the Hoo er residence. It looks identical to the Hoo er house. Same buried mat, sizeable icicle, diamond-shaped window. Surely, it's not the same. His are the only footprints around. Nobody has been coming or going since the storm. His hand is halfway to the doorbell when he remembers it won't work.

"Hello?" Bryce says, knocking loudly. "Anyone home?"

Inside is nothing. He feels the emptiness of the place. There's no need to knock again. If he hurries, Bryce figures, he can visit one more home before it's too late. "But that's it," he mutters, hunching his shoulders and shuffling along the road. The farther he gets from his truck, the deeper the accumulation of snow.

Another front porch. Another knock. Winded, his breath comes quicker now and when he hollers, "Hello?" his voice is phlegmy and hoarse. "Anyone home?"

On his way to the next house, Bryce wonders if he's made a mistake. The darkness and distance has swallowed up his truck. Perhaps he should have gone to the Hoo ers' other next-door neighbor instead of trekking all this way backward. He's practically to the highway, he thinks, but can't be sure. "This one is the last one," Bryce says as he high steps through the snow.

In memory, light and time don't obey the same rules. That summer, Bryce recalls as he walks, darkness fell out of nowhere. Or maybe a storm cloud blotted out the sky. In an instant the sun-bedazzled fish was dull and gray. Its ashen scales were torn to ribbons by feasting flies. Bryce could feel the shiver of maggots gorging on fish innards. The bluegill spun in a tight circle. Those wet bugs didn't even know they were awaiting wings.

And the boy just stood there. Still, he stood. Why would a boy purposefully stand there and watch it die? Did he get some kind of perverse pleasure out of torturing animals? Was his face awash in devilish glee?

Bryce doesn't bother to call out when he gently knocks on the door of the next house or the next house. At the next house, he stands on the porch, shivering, and can't remember why he's there. Can't remember if he has already knocked.

Then he hears the sudden explosion of barking from inside.

When the door opens, a man wearing flannel pajamas greets Bryce awkwardly while trying to prevent two blond Cocker Spaniels from escaping. "Settle down!" the man scolds. He edges himself outside to stand on the stoop and closes the front door. On his feet are fur-lined brown slippers. Though it's too dark to make out features, the man's eyebrows are thick and arched quizzically. A dim wash of light, possibly from a lantern in the foyer, squeezes out the front window.

"Sorry," the man says with a reedy voice. "What can I do for you?"

"Well," Bryce says, clearing his throat. "I was plowing the road and…"

"You get stuck?" the man interrupts. When the man speaks, his neck twitches. The quick spasm reminds Bryce of a small bird on a high branch.

"No. I was just doing my job when…"

"You ran out of gas?"

"No," Bryce says, shaking his head to clear away the fog. "I hit a dog."

"Oh. That's bad."

"I wanted to tell the owner."

"Mine are accounted for, thankfully."

"I didn't do it. I mean, it was already dead. Frozen and buried in snow. I couldn't possibly have seen it."

"I'm sure you couldn't. Probably not your fault. What kind was it?"

"A Shepherd, I think."

"You think?"

"I'm not sure."

"Did you retrieve the collar?"

"I never found the head."

"No head?"

"Yeah. I mean, no. It was buried."

"Hmm," the man says. It's impossible for Bryce to read his expression. The twitch returns with a sudden, violent spasm. "You sure it was a dog?"

"Pretty sure. What else could it be?"

"Could have been a boy."

"Excuse me?"

"I said it could have been a wolf. Sometimes they come out of the woods over there," he says, gesturing to the trees in the distance.

"I hadn't thought of that," Bryce says. He runs his gloved hand across his numb face. "Wild animals don't just freeze, though."

"A wounded one would."

"Wounded how? Like, shot?" Even squinting, Bryce can't make out the man's features.

"Hey," the man says, nodding at Bryce's hand, "you're bleeding."

Bryce's left-hand glove is stained red. The wound on his sliced finger has reopened. He has no idea how long it's been bleeding. Probably a while. There's a substantial blotch.

"Unless that's animal blood?"

Maybe it's a trick of the wind or a damp spot in the hollow of his ears but the man's voice sounds considerably deeper. The dogs inside are silent. And yet Bryce can hear a low, rhythmic panting which seems to be coming from the house itself.

"I should get going."

"You better come inside," the man says, opening the door. Bryce expects the dogs to burst out, but they're gone. "I can bandage your hand."

"No," Bryce says, taking a step backward. "I'll be fine."

"You sure?"

"Yeah, I've got to get home."

Bryce slips to his knees as he scrambles away. Behind him, the man says, "Watch your step!"

Bryce stands, stumbles again on the ice, and finally finds his feet.

"You're going the wrong way," the man calls out. "Turn around."

Bryce ignores the man and charges forward the same way he charged out of the bushes that summer. He planned on tapping the boy on the shoulder, spinning him around and explaining, *We don't do that!* Shake some sense into the kid.

Instead, a dollop of murk slipped from Bryce's head into his heart, which may have been why he roughly cupped his hand over the boy's mouth. To teach him a lesson. To show him what it's like to be without breath. Feel what the fish felt.

The boy writhed and kicked and bit—*goddamnit*—it was difficult to keep him still. Bryce had no choice but to use force. To get a firm grip on the nape of his neck—scruff him—and submerge his head in the pond. The boy's face went under. Bryce could see his own visage mirrored back in the agitated reflection: his flushed cheeks hot with anger, chin smeared with mud, eyes two black dots.

The idea, as Bryce recalls, was to hold the boy under for twenty seconds—any boy can hold his breath that long—and then let him free. No real harm done. Lesson learned. But every time he'd count—*one Mississippi, two Mississippi, three Mississippi*—the boy would thrash violently, free his head, and gulp up more air. Then Bryce would have to start all over again: *one Mississippi, two Mississippi, three Missi…quit…fight…ing…me…*

It took forever to get to twenty.

A lot of time has passed since then. The pond is iced over now. Bryce has no memory of the boy biting his hand or if he released him. He's not sure where the kid went. He could still be there, frozen in time and place. His memories are so slippery they make his head spin. Was he the boy thinking he was the man or else the man imagining he was the boy?

When Bryce returns to the county road, it's gone. Drifting snow has buried it. There are no traces of his footprints. It's impossible to say whether the truck is this way or that way. Night is here, that's for sure. The snow has stopped falling. The sea of unblemished white makes the dark darker. Wind gusts in ceaseless waves unbroken by the empty expanse of field.

Far off in the distance, Bryce sees a pinprick of light. It winks once and disappears. Then it returns with a partner. Two lights, Bryce thinks. Like headlights from a snowplow bearing down. When he blinks, another faint glow appears. And still another. It could be flashlights from a rescue party searching for him. Could be the power slowly crackling on. Might be a pack of wolves advancing.

What Bryce sees are stars. He has stumbled again and is now lying flat on his back. It happened so fast; one second he was standing, and now he is not. The brightest stars puncture the dissipating cloud cover. The light has traveled a great distance across vast, dead space.

In that quiet repose Bryce remembers the prayer he was whispering just as his uncle came upon him, furious, and dunked his head beneath the surface of the pond. He'd said, *Lord, give this little guy a second chance. He doesn't deserve to die.* And, come to think of it, the bluegill did shudder back to life. Bryce should know. He had his eyes wide open underwater for a long twenty seconds. He can see it now: a quick silver flash diving down into the dark.

YOUR NEAREST EXIT MAY BE
BEHIND YOU

US AIRWAYS BOMBARDIER CLASS CRJ200, flight number 1745, departs from O'Hare International ahead of schedule—7:22 p.m.—en route to LaGuardia International. Upon the regional jet, including crew, are thirty-four people. The pilot's name is Jennifer Hughes; copilot is Simon Wentworth. Though all the passengers have names, identities evaporate after clambering into their assigned seats. In an aircraft it's more efficient to categorize passengers by a number and letter combination. There are two people named John on board and only one of them is seated in 14C. There are also three people named Sam (a man, a baby, and a teenage girl). It will be confusing when someone starts shouting, "Sam! Sam! Sam!" rather than, "9D! 9D! 9D!"

Winds are a moderate fifteen miles an hour out of the west. At cruising altitude—forty-one thousand feet—Captain Hughes decides it's safe for folks to unfasten seatbelts and use the lavatory, as necessary. 4C, the passenger sitting in the fourth-row aisle, becomes Frederick Templeton, a large man with a small bladder, when he struggles out of his seat and teeters toward the bathroom. 14B, wearing a Yankees hat, becomes who he is—Ben Spectacle—when he stands to fetch a paperback from a carry-on he stowed in the overhead compartment. Trina Roberson, the flight attendant, reminds him to be careful when opening the bin as items might have shifted.

There are other things to keep in mind. Stay buckled when seated. Don't smoke. Destroying the lavatory smoke detectors is prohibited by law. In the event of a decompression, an oxygen mask will automatically appear in front of you. Seat cushions can be used as flotation devices. Locate your nearest exit. It may be behind you.

Roughly an hour into the flight, just as passengers are starting to doze off, the baby begins to cry. Babies on planes are worse than snakes. At least rattlers quit fussing after they've bitten. 9D is in a car seat buckled into the airplane seat. A lollipop-yellow baby blanket is draped over the carrier, creating a cocoon within which baby is nestled. The crying commences when 9C peeks inside and decides to pick 9D up. Baby, in mother's arms, becomes Sam.

9C, mom, feels bad. She doesn't want to cause a scene. As she meanders up and down the aisle, she apologizes to the agitated gawkers in nearby rows. She desperately hums the "Hush Now, Baby," ditty.

No longer in her seat, 9C is Laura Fisher. She lives in New York City with her husband, who is a computer consultant. When they first met, after a few drinks, and he mentioned his profession, Laura said, "You mean you give advice to robots?" Then she snorted at her own joke—a joke she had to explain to Greg because it was so bad and didn't make sense; he *consults* not *counsels* and there's a difference between a computer and a robot. Greg found Laura's simple humor endearing. Most of the women he knew had the personality of a turnip.

The young family flew to Chicago to visit Laura's parents and Greg returned to New York a week ago.

In Orchard Park, a suburb of Chicago, Sam and Laura stayed in her old bedroom. Her sentimental parents never threw away the crib she used as a baby. They put it right next to her single bed. Greg slept on a pull-out couch in the living room. Laura was surprised how much her old room looked like it used to. Ordinarily, when they visited, Laura and Greg stayed in a hotel. It had been fifteen years since she'd actually slept in her room. The cotton-ball clouds she glued to the ceiling were still there, though they had darkened with dust. Faint pencil marks in the closet doorframe marked her ascending height. She marveled at how little she had grown since she last measured back in high school. The fist-shaped red stain on the carpet near the window where she spilled nail polish was still there. Beneath the bed, in a plastic bin, was her collection of dolls. When Sam got cranky, she'd set the baby in the crib, grab a figurine, and put on a little performance. Mixed in with her dolls were a few from her much older sister—more like an aunt—who moved out of the house when Laura was four years old. Brooke loved Baby Forever dolls, made with soft vinyl skin and chubby arms, tiny wrinkled feet, and a bellybutton slit. The one that soothed Sam best was named Destiny Raine. Each doll came with its own birth certificate. Destiny's was crumpled and creased in the back of the bin.

Now, so far from home, Laura sternly whispers, "Quit it, Sammy bear. Hush now. Everyone's staring." She clutches the infant to her chest, nearly to smother. Babies can feel their mother's heartbeat and will relax when you position them just right which, apparently, she is failing to do. Though her parents told her otherwise, Laura knows she's a terrible mother. She feels it in her bones. It comes naturally for some women. In time, Laura will figure it out. She'll adapt. Right now, though, she can't think straight. The baby screech is on maximum volume. The blood in her veins feels sharp. It pricks the tips of her fingers from inside. The nape of her neck perspires. She grows lightheaded and, without her consent, slips into a detached, removed-from-the-moment state—that feeling you get when you're not sure if you are who you think you are.

The only reason she doesn't faint is the fear of spilling and shattering Sam. Laura doesn't need that kind of attention, to appear an even greater fool than she is. All the eyes beneath personalized over-head lights skewer her. Laura feels like screaming. Instead, she returns the baby to the seat by the window. Maybe there's something to see out there. Then, miraculously, Sam quits. The crying ceases the moment baby becomes 9D. Passengers first hold their collective breath and then their applause.

"Here," Trina says, handing 9C a cup of water. "It'll be fine."

"Thanks," she says. "It wasn't like this on the flight over."

"Babies cry. Everyone knows that."

"How much farther?"

"Not long," Trina says. "We'll be descending soon."

Outside, the mid-June sun is setting. The vast world is burnt umber. It is the color a chick sees from within its egg beneath the warm incubation light right before it peck, peck, peck, pecks into the world.

Inside, the light is dim. 9C has not slept through the night in a long, long time. She drifts off now, like many others.

Just as you are not really you when you dream, you're also not really you when you fly. Take, for example, the difficulty of pinpointing precisely where you are on a plane. Sure, you're in your seat, next to an annoying man who keeps elbowing you in the gut (and make no mistake, it's intentional), but strip away the steel and plastic and where are you? The plane is a blip on the air traffic control's radar, but a passenger is much smaller. A micro-pixel upon a pulsing cursor. US Airways Bombardier class CRJ200 is blinking along like it should from point A (O'Hare) toward point B (LaGuardia). And you're on the plane. You paid for your ticket. You worked hard for the money. What sacrifices you've made and what price you've paid to sit in 12A, in an exit aisle. You had to nod your head when Trina asked if you would be willing to assume the responsibilities of occupying a seat in this row. Even though you weren't listening and aren't exactly sure what you're supposed to do in the unlikely event of an emergency, you acknowledged that you would try. Try not to die. Not that you want to think about dying. And you don't want to think about where you or your spirit might go. It's hard to wrap your head around an afterworld when you don't even know where you are in this world. Just in the sky. Moving at 488 mph. Even if you could determine where you are right now, you're not there anymore. You're a ghost in the contrail. You're different now because you left behind—at the airport—your friends, family, a job, pets, a tiny strip of dental floss in an otherwise completely empty garbage can at the Sheraton. You wonder if that insignificant thread is enough for the maid to replace with a new liner or if she will leave it in there and hope the next occupant won't discover the blood-stained filament festooned with microparticles of your rotting food bits. You're not sure what you'd do. You're not sure why you should care. The room was small, moldy, overpriced, and it smelled like dog vomit. The next chump who stays there has bigger worries than a harmless string that is or is not in the mauve-colored plastic bathroom receptacle. It's not your concern. You are a passenger with flossed teeth aboard flight 1745 who hears someone toward the front of the plane scream, "Sam! Sam! Sam! Where's Sam?"

Sam, the man, and Sam, the teen, are startled. They're right here. "I'm right here," they say from 5A and 7C, respectively. They are not the Sam in question. It's Mom in 9C who has awoken, alarmed. Milliseconds ago she was dreaming a version of the truth that, though she's not ready to face *now*, she will acknowledge in another millisecond. During her slumbering sojourn through the unconscious, snapshots of reality stained her cerebellum like images of light on a wall from a twirling projector. She saw her dreamself enter her childhood room. There she found the crib. The same one she had once occupied. Inside, two babies. Destiny facing up, Sam facing down. Both still. Then, at the church. The same one she used to attend as a child. The pews were rounded and made of stone. Upon them blurry names and dates. The words—HEAVEN HAS A NURSERY FOR LITTLE ANGELS—etched into the closest granite slab. Mom, Dad, Brooke, and Greg appeared—they were all outside, somehow—huddled beneath black umbrellas slick as beetle backs. Then she was whisked into a white room with a woman who said things she couldn't comprehend. The woman called Sam *Sid* for some reason. When her dreamself opened her mouth to say, *I don't understand what you're trying to tell me*, passenger 9C unpeeled her eyes. Awake, alarmed, and as the tendrils of the dream evaporate, she is jolted into acknowledging that the baby buckled beside her is Destiny Raine wearing Sam's duck-freckled onesie. The Baby Forever doll cries when you pick her up. On her back or stomach, she is silent.

At the precise moment when passenger 9C emits a primitive, pain-laced howl, 10.6 pounds of grief is yanked—*whoosh*—from her body. That's how much Sam last weighed.

The heaviness of Laura's profound loss doesn't just gouge out her personal pain; it also excavates 10.6 pounds of fleshy regret from everyone else on board. Out of each passenger and crew member, unnoticed, fleshy regret oozes onto the floor. It seeps through imperceptible cracks in the plane and escapes into the atmosphere. Once it's outside, the collective anguish gathers together to form a single, boulder-sized agony bomb which streaks toward Earth.

When the plane dips dramatically from the sudden shift in mass, you feel it like everyone else. Your stomach somersaults and plunges roller-coaster style. Impulsively, you reach for the emergency exit handle and push. Then you wonder if you should pull. Then you suspect you've made a mistake. The guy next to you says, "It's just turbulence," but you're not sure if you can trust him. Then you hear a hissing sound; not like a snake hiss, more like a gas leak hiss. You wonder if the plane is leaking. You wonder if everyone is going to die and if it will be your fault. Is this how you will be remembered? Then again, won't oxygen masks appear if the cabin experiences sudden pressure loss? Have they malfunctioned? Have you malfunctioned? Except for the hysterical woman several rows in front of you, everyone else seems fine.

Several sleepy passengers awakened by Laura's lament discover their clothes are loose. Slacks slide. Shirts slip from shoulders. Wedding rings nearly sneak past the knuckle. This odd sensation—instantaneous body-slimming—disorients. Although she's confused, Trina is a pro. She performs the *There, there, there*s on 9C. She removes the doll from the seat and stows it in an overhead bin.

Now that order is restored, many passengers stand up and marvel at their new bodies. Sam Whitmore asks Megan Vale, "Do I look different?" With thinner fingers, Harvey Wilcox lightly touches his wife Wanda's thinner face. Teenager Michelle Zombrowski, in the back row, sets her phone down and unplugs her earbuds. She feels so happy she dances in the aisle next to Barry Munroe, who claps his hands with a billboard smile.

Jennifer Hughes feels different, too. The place where her uncomfortable pilot pants pinch her thighs is gone. Also, the self-condemnation she feels for leaving the bathroom window cracked open to let in fresh air is gone. Months ago her cat pushed past the screen and escaped. She canvassed the neighborhood with REWARD FOR MISSING CAT flyers. On the photocopied paper she included a picture of Icarus—one in which the tom is attentively staring at the camera—and a promise of a reward to anyone who found him. Though she gave it a great deal of thought, Jennifer didn't specify the monetary amount of the reward. Every number seemed too low. How could she put a value on his companionship? As the days and weeks went by and the flyers were worn down by weather, she grew more and more despondent. A few minutes ago, she was thinking about creating new flyers with a different picture and an outrageous amount—five thousand dollars, a number that might motivate strangers. At that price, surely people would scour the neighborhood. Now, though, Jennifer feels unburdened. The journey toward forgiveness is suddenly over. She realizes that she has somehow been absolved. Now she can focus on the positive memories: snuggling on the couch, watching dead leaves scuttle along the sidewalk outside, sharing a tuna fish sandwich, shredding tissue paper into a magnificent cloud of confetti. Icarus was irreplaceable, true, but the animal shelter is full of countless purring possibilities.

"What the hell was that?" copilot Wentworth asks. He's not even thinking about recently upsetting his mother.

"I don't know," Jennifer answers.

"Turbulence?"

"Maybe."

"Do you feel different?"

"Difficult to say. At this altitude your mind can play tricks on you." Jennifer tries to shake away her calm contentedness and concentrate on the darkening sky. She places both hands on the yoke. "Illuminate the fasten seatbelt signs," she says. "Prepare for landing."

———

In the morning, the stories commence. News of the unexplained phenomena aboard US Airways Bombardier class CRJ200 flight number 1745 crackles across the airways and rockets through cyberspace. Everyone wants to know how they, too, can lose 10.6 pounds of fat—and feel super great afterward—just by taking a short domestic flight.

For a while, before everyone forgets, how the weight was lost and where it went will be discussed. Some people speculate aliens. Extraterrestrials zapped the flesh for special tests. The exact amount—10.6 pounds—is part of a mathematical equation which alientologists are feverishly decoding. Others suspect the government is using a secret fat-blasting cloud on unsuspecting citizens. Once they've ironed out the kinks, they're going to fog the public in an effort to combat the ever-bulging obesity epidemic. Christians claim God just wanted to take a little pinch of His creation for who knows what reason. It's not for any of us to say. Nonbelievers declare it a hoax. Passengers are in on the scam. They're getting some kind of monetary payment or at least frequent flying bucks.

If a group of skeptics climbed into a van, drove the curving gray roads through the Pine Creek Gorge in Wellsboro, Pennsylvania, to the remote cabin on the edge of the state park, and if they crowded around the entrance and peered in, they would struggle to explain what they saw: an enormous man lying on the floor beneath a jagged and sizable rent in the roof, eyes pinched shut and bulbous head thrashing from side to side as if trying to ward away a colony of demons. If, somehow, the facts were provided to these awestruck naysayers—last night, the forty-two-year-old man weighed 185.5 pounds, and this morning he weighs 545.9 pounds—the sudden additional 360.4 pounds absorbed by the man would be inexplicable to them. Even if you handed one of the doubters a calculator so he or she could multiply the number of passengers on flight 1745 times the purported loss of weight and then added that number to what the man used to weigh, they still would not believe you. Everyone knows you can manipulate numbers.

———

Zig Botham had a bad night. He doesn't know what hit him. Like everyone else, Zig has occasionally felt a hollow ache, a festering lack, and has vaguely waited for something to fill him up and give his life purpose. This, though, is not what he had in mind.

Every summer Zig uses the cabin as an art studio where he can work on his landscape paintings. During the year he rents an apartment near Wellsboro High, where he teaches tenth grade. The cabin is *unplugged*, as Zig likes to tell his colleagues; no internet, no telephone, no distractions. Last night, he heard something screaming from the sky. Then the roof exploded and he was struck in the chest by an enormous gelatinous mass. The crushing impact knocked him from the bed to the floor, where he was consumed by the blobby bomb. At the time, he'd hoped he was having a nightmare. He figured he'd wake up, do a few jumping jacks, take a quick jog in the clean air, enjoy a cup of coffee, and then work on a cluster of star-shaped mountain laurels he is sketching beside a meandering and sun-dappled stream. That hope has faded. He's awake and can barely breathe. His many chins constrict his esophagus. His raspy breath is labored and loud; each wheezing gasp is a temporary victory. If he doesn't find the strength to roll over, he'll surely suffocate.

Worse than all these pounds he's mysteriously absorbed is the sudden and severe depression that fogs Zig's skullscape. There are so many things he's never done that he suddenly regrets. He thinks, *I wish I never told Amy I loved her.* Although Zig does not know anyone named Amy, he can vividly picture himself sitting on the edge of the unmade bed with his arm around a sobbing middle-aged woman. She just professed her feelings, to which he didn't immediately respond. It's not like he doesn't care. He certainly doesn't want her to be sad. So, gently, he coaxes her hands from her face, brushes aside the frazzled tangle of blond hair, and says, "Don't cry. I love you, too."

Then, in a flash, he thinks, *I'll win the Rolex back.* Zig doesn't gamble, but he's transported to the poker table excited by a full boat—jacks over kings—and then devastated when the heavy-lidded bald man sitting beside him reveals four deuces. His chest tightens. Blood pressure soars. He's a bad bump away from a cardiac arrest. Next he's whisked into an alleyway. He's rifling through a purse he just snatched from an oblivious woman chattering on her phone near a park bench. Inside the bag—including credit cards, thirty-seven dollars, and a pair of silver earrings—is an inhaler the woman probably needs when she suffers a panic attack triggered, for instance, by having her purse stolen. *I should have returned the inhaler*, he thinks, as he ditches the purse and slinks down the sidewalk.

The anguish of strangers leeches into Zig's bloodstream and pumps melancholy in black waves through his elephantine heart. He cannot combat the relentless barrage of remorseful memories: *I didn't write that A essay on* Hamlet; *I should have gone to the prom with Henry; why did I give her the car keys when she was clearly drunk; I wish I didn't burn every single photograph of Morgan; why did I tell Cindy the neighborhood was safe; I can't tell Mom I returned that hideous shirt she bought for my birthday; I wasn't working late at the office; I'll never see a dime of that money I lent Alex; this tattoo will never fade; I lied when I said I'd stick around in sickness and in health; why did I criticize Richard for spilling my coffee on the kitchen floor before heading to work so many Septembers ago; I shouldn't have skipped that last AA meeting; I'm the one who forgot to lock the front door; why couldn't I keep my big mouth shut; if I'd closed the window Icarus would still be waiting for me at home; my baby is gone.*

Zig's organs bulge. Stretch marks carve a map upon his enormous belly. Inside, a million bad decisions gestate. His pores clog with dank sweat. He is at a loss for what to do now. Even if he knew the truth, what would he do? Track down the flight crew and passengers aboard flight number 1745 and deliver the burdens to their rightful owners? Nobody would reclaim them. That baggage is lost. Besides, everyone is busy gaining weight from other agonies.

Zig thrashes his head from side to side until his gaze falls on a shoebox tucked beneath his bed. He recognizes it immediately and wills himself to stay still and focus. It's a box his mother gave him fifteen summers ago, when she visited him at the cabin one early afternoon. The two sat at a picnic table beneath the shade of a poplar while Mom explained what she wanted Zig to do. She'd read an article in *Cosmopolitan* that suggested several ways to bring your family together when you felt it was drifting apart.

"You think we're drifting apart?" Zig asked.

"Probably not," Mom said. "But I want us to do this anyway. It'll be fun."

What she wanted Zig to do was dredge up thoughts and feelings about his parents that he couldn't express aloud and put them in a box. Once everyone in the family contributed, they would all sit down and share.

"No judgments," Mom said.

"And Dad agreed to do this?" Zig asked.

"He said he would if you would."

"I don't have any feelings I can't express to you and Dad in person. Maybe we should just have coffee this weekend."

"No," Mom said, panicked. "The article insists we reflect alone and share together. That's how the bond strengthens. It'll be easy, Zig. Just write a poem or make a picture." She set the shoebox on the table and slid it over to her son. "What I did is write letters to you and your father and even my future self. And you know, it felt good."

"I don't know," Zig said.

"Just try. For me."

Zig did try. He drew a portrait of his mother with a yellow bow in her hair. It only took him a few hours. He folded it and placed it in the box. Then he sketched a self-portrait, which wasn't difficult at all; it was an assignment he always gave his students. It only took him an afternoon. He put it in the box, too. Then he tried to draw his father's face. For some reason, he couldn't remember what his dad looked like, exactly. He knew what he looked like, of course, but he had trouble matching the actual man with the impression of the man. He and his father had a decent relationship. Nothing complicated. Before Dad grew too old they fished and hiked and threw the baseball around. They never talked about art or anything, which was fine by Zig. Dad was a stoic auto mechanic who stressed the importance of hard work. He often had grease on his face and so, in the portrait, Zig added a few dark streaks on his cheeks along with wispy hair, a hooked nose, and a broad chin. Then he worked on the eyes. Right away he knew he was in trouble. Every set he drew felt off; too crooked, too severe, too blue. In the end, he decided to draw his father's eyes closed. It looked like Dad was asleep. It also looked like Dad was dead.

By the time Zig ripped the portrait from the sketchpad and jammed it into the shoebox, summer was over. He returned to teaching. In the fall, his mother checked on Zig's progress and asked him if he had finished. "No pressure," she said, "but I'd really like your father to participate soon." Zig lied and told her he'd forgotten it at the cabin, and with school underway it might take him a while to fetch it. Then in the winter, when Mom asked him again, Zig told her he'd retrieve it when the snow relented. When she asked in the spring, Zig had the flu and he promised he'd get it when he felt well. In June, Zig's mother filed for divorce and moved to Florida. She never asked about the box again.

Zig shoved it under the bed and it faded from his memory. Since then, the years have chewed up Zig's father, who lives out quiet days in the Silver Valley nursing home.

Until now, Zig never considered that he contributed to his mother's leaving. He figured she and Dad had simply grown out of love.

It occurs to him now that *he* might have been part of the problem. When they were all younger, they had been like a circuit. The box of expressions was supposed to provide a jolt of electricity to jumpstart the good times. It was Zig who broke the chain.

Zig desperately wobbles back and forth. Then, miraculously, he rolls onto his side. He fishes under the bed for the shoebox and clutches it to his chest. He can see the front door. Encouraged, he squirms across the scuffed floor. It's not easy to squeeze onto the creaking porch, but he manages. He finds the strength to lift himself to hands and knees. His old Dodge is in the unpaved driveway. He hoists himself up. Beside his car, he rests. His tender skin feels like it's melting in the heat. Slathered in a sheen of sweat, he shimmies behind the wheel. The car groans and tilts, but it drives. He can, if he stays focused, motor to Silver Valley and park.

At his destination, unwedging himself from the driver's seat nearly kills him. He leans heavily on the hood and gathers strength. Then, ready or not, he walks. Every precarious baby step is a gift. The automatic double doors leading to the lobby part. Inside, Zig ignores the flustered receptionist. Using the wall for support, he trundles down the hall past 12A, 13B, and 14C until, at last, he looms in his father's doorway.

Zig's father had been napping in the rocking chair next to the window. He'd just now been dreaming something he forgets the moment he opens his eyes. There, huffing at his door, is an enormous man he doesn't recognize. His hair is matted, eyes wild, mouth and chin spackled with slobber. When the stranger holds out an old shoebox like an offering, the father leans forward and squints.

"Boy," he says, confused. "Is that you?"

Zig feels the weight of the box. It is heavier than he thinks it should be, and for a second he wonders if there's something more inside. He crams himself into the small room and stands beside the single bed. When he sets the box on the mattress, he feels ten pounds lighter. "Here," he says. "Mom wanted me to give this to you."

The father's quizzical look deepens into a scowl. Sunshine slants through the window and turns the room crimson. "Your mother?" he asks, his voice rising in pitch. "Is she here? You should have called. What happened to you?"

"I can't explain," his son says, "but I'll try." Although he has every intention of puzzling through his affliction with his father, Zig's assaulted heart has other plans. He gasps once and then crashes to the floor.

———

Zig survives. Paramedics are able to defibrillate his heart back into motion and race him to the hospital, where doctors do what doctors do: poke, prod, and speculate. Once he's stable, a team of specialists interested in medical anomalies zoom in from Philadelphia to have a look. Zig Botham becomes patient 69538.

Experts discard a number of possible explanations for the sudden weight gain—diabetes, water retention, loss of sleep, stress, kidney problems—and settle on Cushing's disease. They send samples to the lab and await test results.

In terms of patient 69538's insistence that something came "screaming from the sky" and suddenly "consumed" him, that can be explained by psychologists. Sounds can be deceiving. Isn't it more likely the "scream" came from patient 69538? It's a classic case of projection: when we assign our pain to an external body, we can avoid facing our own internal turmoil. As for physical damage to the cabin, sometimes individuals with psychotic disorders will do something— say, blow a hole through a roof with a shotgun—without retaining any memory of having done such a thing. Although no weapon was found in the cabin, the human mind is just as capable of hiding a physical object as it is of sublimating repressed trauma.

All of that seems plausible to you. You read an article about the curious case of Zig Botham and his sudden weight gain but didn't draw any connection between him and what happened to you and everyone else aboard flight number 1745.

After deplaning in LaGuardia that night, you hit the bathroom and then made your way to the street to await a cab. The evening was humming with light and noise. Standing in line, checking messages on your phone, you noticed someone familiar loading items into a mid-sized gray sedan. It was the woman who freaked out on the plane. She was easy to remember. Even now, if you try, you can still hear the sound of her pain. The man she was with crammed a stroller into the backseat before hustling behind the wheel. The woman slid into the passenger seat and buckled up. She caught you staring and held your gaze with red-glazed and icy-blue eyes. Her piercing glance made you consider your shoes.

Then the car began to pull away and you noticed the bag sitting on the curb. For a moment, you hesitated. Though you couldn't recollect them, you knew there were rules about unattended baggage. Probably passengers forgot items on curbs all the time. A professional would know what to do. Or, you thought, when she realized she left the bag—it was small, dotted with purple flowers, and probably a carry-on—she'd have her husband circle back. If not, she could contact US Airways and have them deliver it.

Then again, she could have left the bag behind on purpose. Was there something dangerous inside? A bomb? Drugs? Was it left for you? Were you supposed to do something?

As you stepped out of line and jogged ahead, your pants slipped down your hips. You had to pull them up when you fetched the woman's bag. "Wait!" you shouted, though there was no way for her to possibly hear you. "Wait!" You waved your arms as her car merged and disappeared into traffic.

By that time, you had drawn the attention of the crowd. A rash of eyes fell upon you as you stood with the woman's luggage. The strangers were waiting to see what you'd do. They wondered what variety of person you were: the kind that follows through and solves a problem or the kind that walks away. Like them, you weren't sure. If you hadn't leapt into action, you'd be gawking at the person who did. Surely someone would have acted if you hadn't. So what that it didn't work out? It was the thought that counted, and you were done thinking about it.

You moved to return to the back of the line and pretend like nothing happened. But when you dropped the bag on the curb, the baby inside began to cry.

THE SALT LIFE

1.

Upon the beach there is a baby on a blanket. The mother, tired, falls asleep. Or the mother is blitzed and passes out. Or the mother stands and walks away, leaving footprints in the sand.

The June sun blazes. It looks green when the baby stares into it. Then everything looks green for a while because that's how momentary blindness from staring into the sun looks. Green, blotchy, furry along edges. The baby's not old enough to be overly concerned with not seeing.

The father is gone, of course. Please. Fathers are fine ideas. They make neat notions. You can count on their absence when you are a baby on a blanket alone and blinded. When you are older and no longer a baby you will situate Dad on a sliding scale—from hero to villain—and after a while it won't much matter where he falls.

Strangers on a beach don't know what to do with a baby on a blanket blinking and cooing and eating sand. The lifeguard's tanning. Children chase crabs. It's just you now, baby. You're old enough to crawl. You have a few options: scoot toward the street where cars flash silver through the green haze, move one direction or the other along the sand between the road and the ocean, or waddle into the water.

When mother awakens she'll boom. *Missing Baby* will splash across the news. Since everybody was temporarily a baby everyone will temporarily care. Squeeze loved ones. If you have a newborn and you're a mother, recommit to staying awake longer or drinking less. If you are a father, go to church. Then when they find dead, bloated baby: collapse, curse, embrace the numb, and get over it by saying you'll never get over it. Or, when the hapless motorist explains *I thought it was a plastic bag blowing off the curb and by the time I realized...*: hate deeply, then collapse, curse, embrace the numb, and get over it by saying you'll never get over it. Or when baby is found dehydrated and shriveled like a coconut beneath a tuft of sea oats: go after the negligent parents. Curse them. They are abominable. You would never leave a baby untended upon a blanket on the beach.

The baby in its green world waits. It begins to burn, eventually, which is one of the reasons why it ambles toward the sea. There are other reasons: the murmuring surf, the tug of the tide, the tempting lure of distant gulls, or the primordial blood-hum drum-drumming from the saline in the veins.

The ocean is a lullaby—*Hush now baby, don't say a word*—and it knows how to care for an infant. Latch onto this sturdy piece of driftwood. Have fun with it. Float, splash, kick, giggle. Tempt the underwater predators. You are not unlike a wounded mackerel floundering. In the right mouth, you are delicious. Don't worry, though, you won't be eaten. Leave paralyzing fear of the unknown to the feebleminded adults. You, baby, are immortal. The waves deliver you to an undiscovered island where a sympathetic chimpanzee soothes your face with aloe and slakes your thirst with stream water. How fantastic is that monkey's love! Baby, baby, grow loved like that. Be good; do better. And never return. You must stay missing forever in order for us to have hope. To believe there's a second chance. To give meaning—the possibility of finding you, baby—to the slurry of countless regurgitated days.

2.

Gyrating from the roadway vein work—the interstates and county roads—bikers follow concrete tributaries in modest rivulets until they pool together for the bike festival. Upon brilliantly colored metallic steeds or tattered rust-speckled hogs they come. On Victory, on Honda, on Harley and Ducati, on Gold Wing, on Yamaha, BMW and Suzuki—ride momma, ride momma, ride.

They come for the beaches and the nightclubs, the restaurants and the bars. They appreciate the hospitality, the southern charm. They chuckle as they buzz in staccato bursts like wing-clipped wasps along clogged Kings Highway, when they discover that the nagging bit of something lodged in the back row of their molars is a piece of grit from the grits they ate this morning, not a pebbly roadway souvenir. They kickstand their ride and loiter. They admire and bask in admiration. It is not Halloween and they are allowed—encouraged—to dress like pirates. Resplendent in bandanas, facial jewelry, newly branded tats, goatees, with cigars, wallet chains, leather boots, ripped vests, and belt buckles in the shape of skulls, they come.

Helmets are optional. Death is not.

There will be many accidents which will claim many lives. Some bikes will buck their riders—there are a myriad reasons why this happens: the wind, alcohol, rain, inexperience, careless cars, mechanical malfunctions, a once-domesticated now-feral dog bursting from the woods—and the unlucky ones will skid along the hot pavement, popping bones and flaying skin until his or her face has been smeared off.

The timid, shaken family man who has saved up all year for this vacation will be either brave enough or dumb enough to pull to the shoulder, instruct his kids to keep eyes in the car, and take the necessary steps not to the heaping pile of machinery but to the gasping mash of flesh in the median. This is not how he imagined his vacation would commence. Nor does he fully understand the consequences of taking in the stark brutality of the scene. He delivers mail. He accidently swiped a deer once. He has been up close with road kill. He is not trained to rescue and respond. The beginning of the vacation will end now. He will not remember the delicious butter-drenched crab claws from Captain Willy or the leisurely laps in the oceanfront pool after hours when the kids are down and the wife convinces him to sneak away naked for a short while. He will not remember the simple joy that blossoms from spontaneously purchasing a pair of hand-painted smiling coconut faces—he'll joke that they look like his kids—though they will remain in the guest bathroom collecting dust long after his children have grown and drifted to college. And though it is not his fault—the brain's way of identifying with the species through facial recognition is automatic—his commitment to doing what he believes is right when he rolls the body over to investigate and hears the unmistakable whoosh of air escaping lungs issuing impossibly somehow through the faceless smooth contours where features ought to be will permanently scorch his memory bank and haunt him forever.

The family man inquires if the victim is all right because he wants so badly for it to be true. Try as he might, he will not be able to convince his body to hunt for a pulse. Instead, he will stand paralyzed humming "Yankee Doodle Dandy." Just moments ago he and his family had been talking about the lyrics to the ditty. His son wanted to know why and what the dandy called macaroni. "It" refers to what, in the song? The family man did not know. The cap? The feather? The feathered cap? Did they have macaroni and cheese back when the tune was penned? This isn't something the father wants to think about now. He doesn't want to think about macaroni later, at the hotel, when he picks out the stringy bits of sloughed-off flesh pressed into his sneakers. He hums to the almost-corpse until he hears ambulance sirens. Returning to his minivan, the family man tries very hard, for the rest of his life, to keep what he has seen to himself.

Those who want to keep bikers off bikes will stress that *Last year the number of motorcyclists who died…blah, blah, blah.* Freedom never comes for free. Bikers are keenly aware of the cost. They have been patient through the doldrums of winter and the slow blooming of spring. They have pushed through the jobs, the joblessness, the nagging spouses, parents, and loan officers. They've explained why they cannot stop payment on their bike, their baby, their pride and joy. A tiny opportunity at freedom, the kind of liberty that is not measured easily—how can they describe the feeling? The wind in your hair, the pungent smell of the gasoline-infused air, the rattling power of the engine rising up from your legs to your chest…

Bikers know it's better to ride than to talk about riding. All they have to do is, somehow, make it to the summer. And now, here, having been delivered, they are revved up.

3.

Soon as sunrise, tourists pour out of the hotels and sweep onto the sand. With broad straw hats casting shadows over soon-to-be crimson-colored faces, with sunscreen pooling in folds of elastic skin around the jowls, they come. With beach ball heads lolling, sunglassed eyes stinging from the sudden sand blasts, lip-glossed mouths puckered and gaping, already in need of water from plastic bottles branded with state flags and soda cans in *Life's a Beach* koozies, they come. Surveying the horizon for a level patch of sand to claim for the day and erect multicolored umbrellas, they come. In ill-fitting swaths of spandex stretched across bodies that were supposed to be sculpted by now—broken New Year's resolutions—in a sarong, a one-piece, bikini, tankini, triangle top, halter, G-string, banana hammock; leaving nothing to the imagination, they come. Feet wedged into plastic flip-flops purchased at a discount from Wings, Eagles, Bargain Beachwear, Beach Bumz, places they'll revisit for shot glasses, hermit crabs, towels, T-shirts, collectable spoons, shell-shaped picture frames, taffy, ships in bottles, keychains, bamboo wind chimes, rubber dolphins, toothpick holders, lanyards, box kites—souvenirs to be divvied out to second cousins, colleagues, aunts, carpool neighbors, in-laws—they come.

With disease and rancor, children and snorkels, geographic pride and southern stereotypes, with the latest cameras, in eco-friendly minivans, with recommendations from family friends, for one-night stands, tattoos, kamikazes, oysters on the half shell, the aquarium, strip clubs, golf courses, cigar bars, Ferris wheels, water slides, pirate shows, fireworks, baby alligators, the shag, ghost tours, helicopter rides, deep-sea fishing, parasailing, gambling boats, ladies' night, tanning salons, ponies, outlets, with maxed-out credit, foreclosed homes, tuition debt, a philosophy on tipping, with skepticism, fear, an uncanny emptiness inside, cataracts, tumors, lottery tickets, budding affairs, pending divorces, quickie gazebo marriages under lilac-seared sunsets on litter-strewn beaches, they come.

In vans and buses. Under the weather. Pleading for a second chance. With and without dogs. No intention of leaving. Away from the law. Careening, doddering, sashaying, limping from the air-sweetened lobbies across the hot sand and into the drink. My lord, they come with insatiable thirst. What can be done, what will be done; they come, they come, they come.

4.

A father and his son play baseball on the beach. Other than a hunched loner with a beach bag watching the sunset upon a blanket, a silhouette like a boulder in the last of the light, they are alone. Nobody's in the water, which is what they've waited for. The son, ten years old, stands poised and ready just out of reach of the waves, facing the sea. He keeps his elbow up. Legs bent. Eye on the ball. The tip of the aluminum bat fidgets like a scorpion's tail, just like it should.

Dad's knee deep in water. His feet are sinking into the sand. He's got an orange beach pail filled with baseballs which he holds by the handle in his left hand. Together, they etched home plate into the sand. All that remains is the pitch.

The father has been preparing for this moment for a long time. He's been scheming since Pittsburgh on the drive down for their vacation. Last year the boy moved from machine-pitch baseball to human-pitch. His son struggled. It's one thing to hit a ball that follows the consistent trajectory of an automated X300 Pitch-o-matic, and another to slug the erratic flight from a human hand. He's had difficulty making contact with the ball. He'll step into the batter's box with a head of confidence that always wavers before the baseball pops the catcher's mitt. The boy's inclination is to step back, flinch, and lower his shoulder every single time, regardless of what the pitcher is dealing.

"It's natural to be afraid of the ball," Dad said, and then continued saying other things—things fathers say to tentative kids. "You've got to be assertive."

The father had also been a meek son, and to regard his son as a version of himself intimidates him into considering how his own dad, the boy's grandfather, might behave. Dad wondered what Dad would do and decided on this.

"It doesn't hurt. Be a man. Toughen up. I'll buy you ice cream. Don't be a girl." All that Dad said, and more.

Boy listened but it didn't matter a whit. Still carried a quivering lip. Sloped shoulders. Distributed too much weight on his heels; a kid ready to step backward and concede defeat before Pitch wound up.

Last season, in the stands, Dad ground his teeth and sweated. Mom lightly touched his knee. She said, "Come on, Tyler! You can do it!" and when he struck out—without even swinging the bat—said, "Good try! Next time, baby!"

Dad sometimes encouraged, too, from the stands. "Almost," he'd shout. Or, "Buck up, champ." Some such shit he never remembered his own Pop saying. He'd study the better boys—Mack, Buster, Cal, Sonny—and ask Ty, after the game, if he'd been watching. Paying attention to his better teammates. "You see how Rocky hung in there? Waited for his pitch. Kept his shoulder squared. Then, boom!" Dad would say and then sock his son in the bicep with more force than he intended but less than he wanted.

Boy saw, boy felt; bruised.

Now, here, it's twilight. Mom's back in the hotel room in her bathrobe watching *Lifetime*. Just the boys, the sand, the stranger, the rising moon, and the onlooking ocean.

Earlier at dinner Tyler asked, "You want me to hit the balls into the water?" Dad was deliberately drinking too much wine despite the wife-scowls. Wife is Mom who believes serious boys grow into conscientious men. Baseball is just a game. You play for fun. Don't enjoy it, quit.

Dad gulped a bottle so that he'll be able to say, later, "I'm sorry. I might have been a little tipsy." Then, "I'm sorry," again, in the morning. Maybe a third time—on the quiet drive back home—strike one, strike two, strike...

"It'll float," Dad said. "Tide'll bring them back." He'd burped discreetly into his napkin. "Unless you really get a hold of one and knock it to Europe!"

Boy's here then, happy. None of his friends have ever hit baseballs into the ocean willy-nilly like this. Dad's got a sloppy smirk on his face and he's loose. Boy likes Dad best when he's loose. So far, the vacation has been fantastic. He never wants to head for home.

Dad's got six baseballs in the bucket. The first few he throws slow. Boy misses, fouls, and then miraculously crushes one. Whistles into the breakers. It's the kind of hit that almost makes Dad second-guess what he does next.

Dad winds up and wings a fastball at his kid's head. It's too dark for the boy to really see what's coming his way until it's too late. He'll take it on the chin.

This is what it means to love, Dad tells himself as he wades dramatically to shore to comfort his son, which is the kind of thing he believes his own father might think.

And maybe he's right. Tyler, after the tears and confusion, might love like this, too.

5.

The Sea Turtle Patrol has been monitoring a stretch of sand on the south side where loggerheads have nested. The conditions are better, with fewer people and less unnatural light and noise from hotels. Tonight, nearly midnight with a bulbous moon, they're hoping to witness an emergence.

The mother makes the nest so it's wide at the bottom and narrow at the top. When the turtles hatch, they flap flippers around like crazy. Sand trickles down. Hatchlings ride an elevator of sand to the surface.

Once the babies are above ground, they're vulnerable. The phosphorescent glow of the whitecaps on the waves draws the hatchlings to the sea. Sometimes, lights from hotels and passing cars disorient the young and they'll scuttle the wrong way. Often they become pancakes on the pavement.

Even if they're heading in the right direction, there are dangers: ghost crabs, raccoons, gulls, foxes. Holes in the sand that children have dug in the daytime are a problem. If a tiny turtle slips inside it can become trapped and charred to a crisp in the daytime heat.

Without the Sea Turtle Patrol, the baby loggerheads would be in big trouble. This group prides itself on having 100% into-the-sea success rate. No hatchling under their watchful eyes has ever expired before entering the water. Once they're in the ocean, the babies are on their own.

The only person who is not staring with rapt attention at the nesting site is the youngest member of the patrol, Sandra, a fourteen-year-old girl who hates to be called Sandy. Her parents are sea turtle activists. The six members of the patrol who could make it tonight are all wearing sea-green-colored windbreakers which have small, dark-green-colored turtles dotting the fabric. When the wind picks up their jackets ripple like flags.

Sandra is the only one who sees, along the waterline, a small figure break from the surf and stumble onto land. For a hopeful moment, Sandra imagines the creature is a sea monster draped in ropey seaweed. Or a castaway from a shipwrecked yacht. Maybe a merman. A diminutive somnambulist. She hurled a message in a Snapple bottle into the sea last year—*Someone rescue me!*—and perhaps this is her hero.

Sandra doesn't bother to draw her parents' attention to the person. She's certain they'd say he's a vagrant drunk. They'd enumerate reasons why she must always remain vigilant on this part of the beach at this time of the night. She decides to keep her mouth shut. Soon, the person staggers up the shore and into darkness. Turning her attention to the nest, she waits with the others for the eggs to hatch.

6.

Friday mornings, before sun-up, the old men slowly totter toward the sea with their fishing rods and fold-out chairs tucked precariously akimbo beneath liver-spot spackled and hairless limbs. These men—ten or so, give or take, depending on who's able to awaken—are members of the Anglers Club. They fish on the south side where licenses are relaxed. They've been fishing license-less for years without ever receiving a ticket.

They work quietly, for the most part. They're not here to gossip. There will be time to exchange lies after the lines have been cast and there's nothing to do but worry over the dipping tips of the poles and fidget with tackle. Now, though, in the semi-dark, they'll divide their work. The bait-catchers—ones with the best knees and backs— cast nets into the surf and collect minnows. The strongest few hammer PVC pipes into the sand where they can holster the rods. The nimble-fingered men with the mildest arthritis tie slipknots and toil at the rigging.

Each man wades into the water alone and casts his fate into the wave chop. The heart leaps as the looping line lashes the pungent morning air.

When the sun crests it'll find a platoon of fishermen. This time of year, when the ocean's as warm as bath water, they catch blues, reds, whiting, or spots. These fish clean easy and taste fine battered and cooked for the Friday Night Fish Fry they'll attend, after an afternoon nap, at the rec center.

Sometimes, one of them will hook a flounder as wide as a manhole and it will require a group effort to heave it upon shore. The thought of cutting the line before tugging the flopping thing to the wet sand does not cross their minds. If you've hooked something, you reel it in. There's nothing confusing about fishing.

If they dredge something up from the sea they don't want—a barracuda, black-tip shark, stingray—the strongest men fetch the PVC-driving hammers and whack it to death so they can retrieve their hooks. Sometimes the men with nimble fingers will slice the bludgeoned catch to ribbons to be used as bait. Before they do, it's important to consult with the bait-catchers. Feelings have been hurt in the past. Quarrels are common.

More often than not, it's best to heave the carcass back into the ocean.

7.

The old woman unpeels the banana and mouths it suggestively to her husband. This is a joke between them. Since losing her teeth, she's all gums and dentures. They've laughed about what great pleasure a toothless blowjob would give the old man. He hasn't been able to get it up in years and the erection medicine causes his lips to swell like a monkey. So, she fellates the banana and they both enjoy it.

The beach chairs they're sitting on are rusted. In places, the cross-stitched weave has come undone. The two are finishing their lunch. The sun is directly overhead. They're too old to care about sun block. Their elephant skin is blotched with tacky patches of melanoma.

Tourist season is their favorite time of the year. They angle their chairs toward the pier and people watch.

"Bob's heading home," the woman says after she has swallowed the banana. She under-hands the peel into the surf.

The old man shades his eyes. He spies Bob, the fisherman, arms loaded with an array of poles and tackle, teetering along the beach. "I believe he's whistling," the old man offers.

"Must have done well."

"*Yankee Doodle Dandy.*"

"You can't hear what song he's whistling."

"How about you come over here and yankee my doodle, Dandy?" The old man lifts and then lowers his eyebrows in rapid succession.

"Don't you get fresh."

"Fetch yourself another nana."

"Wouldn't you like that?"

"Has its a-ppeal," he says, letting the second syllable linger in his throat.

THE SALT LIFE   71

The woman's phlegmy laugh gives over to a clipped bark.

"It's a dog-eat-dog world," he says.

"I never cared for that expression. Doesn't make a lick of sense."

"Pit bull'd eat a Chihuahua."

"Not without cause. Don't conflate provocation with hunger."

"Pit bull'd eat you, too. Just cause it's bored."

"Bite, maybe. Eat, no."

"Those dogs are related to the T-Rex."

"You're a T-wreck."

"It comes down to mincing. A Chihuahua dog'd eat a minced Pit if you defurred it and mixed it in a bowl with some kibbles. And vice versa, though you'd probably only need to bisect the Chihuahua and leave it in its own bloody mess. Pit bull'd chomp it in two bites."

"That's just gross."

"Yeah, but dogs *will* eat dogs, is my point."

"It's a dumb figure of speech. Dogs don't speak. If they did, they'd tell you to shut up."

"You don't think people'd eat people?"

"Don't be obnoxious."

"You think McDonald's would take a hit if they slipped a morsel of human flesh in their Whoppers?"

"We just ate."

"As I recall, you used to put me in your mouth from time to time."

"Sheet," the woman says, smiling. It's how she swears these days.

"Dog sheet."

"Pigeon sheet."

"Hog sheet."

"Sheep sheet."

"Yankee Doodle Dandy sheet."

Minnows nibble at the discarded banana peel. Up the shore a group of children fight over a shark tooth one boy discovered. The kids don't know how to take turns holding the triangular object. They don't contemplate the significance of the artifact—the fact that they are holding a part of an animal whose brethren swam with dinosaurs. Instead, if they think at all, it's of the slash, rip, tear, and thrash. The kid who discovered it is the smallest and meekest among them. He clutches the tooth in his tiny fists. The others, including his brother, pummel him with earnest punches and dash sand in his eyes.

8.

Midmorning, at low tide, the beach is level, long, and wide. Sands stretch far away.

A group of children decides to create an empire. With Ozymandian hands they construct a sandcastle on the less-populated south side where it won't be trampled. Using plastic buckets and shovels they've constructed the keep, the battlements with ramparts, turrets, and a gatehouse. They're using a fast-food restaurant straw as a pole with an empty Cheetos bag as the flag. A variety of shells festoon the curtain wall: augurs, lettered olives, lightning whelks, cockles, scallops, and arks. A fat gray conch stands guard on the drawbridge.

Once the castle is complete, the children begin digging. At first, they dig because the castle needs a dungeon. After an hour has passed and several of the castle-building children are replaced by children who have grown bored splashing in the shallows, the idea of creating an underground prison cell dissipates. Now, they're digging to China. They're excavating dinosaur bones. They're after Blackbeard's booty.

Lunchtime comes and goes. The patient sun waits for the sunscreen to wear thin so it can burn the tender shoulders of these busy boys and girls.

One petite girl with long limbs eschews implements and digs with her cupped hands. While others chatter excitedly as they make progress (*the hole is big enough to hold an elephant! a helicopter! my*

entire third grade class—with desks!) the girl stays quiet. She keeps
her head down. She concentrates on scooping away, scooping away,
scooping away. Her soft fingertips split and bright red blood dots the
rough, loamy sand.

The children naturally fall into a rhythm. One freckle-faced boy
barks orders and creates an assembly line. Three kids dig (two with
shovels and the determined, unresponsive girl with wounded hands).
Two kids pack the sand into buckets and hoist them to the freckle-
faced boy above who rapidly empties them and tosses them back
down. They make steady progress. Time flies with the sand.

"We could fit an army down here!"

"A pirate ship!"

"Rhode Island!"

The kids might have gone on digging for years and years until
they weren't kids anymore. Eventually, though, a blond-haired boy
has to pee.

"Fine," a boy with a camouflage-decorated bucket says, "go and
come back."

"I can't climb out," the blond-haired boy explains. "It's too high."

This news causes all the kids except the long-limbed girl to pause.
"What do you mean?" they ask. Then they, too, try to escape. When
the freckle-faced boy reaches down to help pull the blond-haired boy
up, he slides in. Then there they are: a half-dozen children in a sizeable pit.

A few kids whimper. Two wail. The silent girl continues to dig.

Some mothers claim they can tell—just *feel*—when their child is
in trouble. Call it a sixth sense. Gut instinct. An invisible umbilical
cord linked to their offspring that can never be severed.

First one, then two, then three mothers arrive. From the lip of
the hole, they stare in horror at their helpless, panicked progeny chattering like featherless chicks.

Mother by mother the women drop into the crater. They lift and tug and push and pull and, with help from the others above, each kid is delivered to the surface.

Only the little girl is left. Her mother is the last to arrive. When she finally does, she calls down to her daughter, "Honey, you can stop now."

"Just a sec," the little girl mutters into the sand.

"Stop, sweetie," Mom stresses through clenched teeth.

"One sec," the girl replies.

Mom, livid, leaps into the dungeon. Her loose bikini top exposes a bit of nipple nobody but the girl sees.

"I said *stop!*" Mom hisses.

"All right," the little girl says. She has dug so far that water is rising up from the floor.

Mom shoves her girl to safety and follows with difficulty.

Now they're all above ground. The mothers gently chastise their children and the children embrace their mothers.

Even the little girl hugs her mom. This comes as a surprise. Mom doesn't understand why her daughter is sort of massaging her lower back. She doesn't know her child is wiping bloody sand into her sun-browned skin. She doesn't know that her daughter was digging a grave for all her sorrow and that it isn't as deep as it needs to be. The mother doesn't know that, since the girl was underground for so long, her eyes are fighting to adjust to the bright sunlight.

The little girl blinks and blinks at the ocean. The hazy horizon looks like an enormous bird flapping its wings. She sees green-colored waves advancing. High tide is approaching. And with it, everything that has drowned.

THE IMMORTAL JELLYFISH

SHORED UP WITH WHAT he believes to be sound intelligence, Clay mounts his metallic-blue ten-speed, punches the code—*1234*—into the keypad, and coasts down the drive. The garage door makes an agonizing clamor upon its descent and for this reason Clay frantically pedals away. Those gears are in desperate need of a good greasing. His father, who visits on odd weekends, always remembers that he has forgotten to bring a can of oil as he waits in his idling red Pontiac Fiero for the door to lift and reveal his trepidatious son slouching in the ever-diminishing shadow vehemently clutching a Star Wars–themed overnight duffle. Today, a Saturday, is not Dad's weekend. The old man is golfing with pals.

Saturdays are busy at *See You Tomorrow*, the multi-purpose future-predicting one-stop-shop in the strip mall down on Atlantic Boulevard where Mom is Madame Galaxy, a reputable astrologer. She likes to check in on her son during lunch break. Clay left a note on the kitchen counter explaining that he is biking to the beach with Jeff and won't be home until five. Cranking like a maniac, the boy's feathered red hair unfeathers in a gust of his own making.

Jeff actually does not factor into the plan. In fact, Jeff can just die and go to hell, as far as Clay is concerned, after yesterday's incident on the tetherball court. At school, Clay likes to eat his lunch outside beneath the bleachers near the basketball courts with a few other ninth graders. The quickest eaters play first. Friday, as he bent down to tie his Reebok sneakers, which chronically come undone, he failed to calculate the elliptical trajectory of the tethered and mostly deflated yellow ball. He has a C- in geometry. Which doesn't matter. Jeff served a stinger that thwapped Clay directly in the ass and caused him to topple over into a pile of color-drained black mulch. All the pimply outcasts in line laughed. So, no Jeff this morning. No fucking Jeff *ever*.

Pompano Beach is a seven-mile bike ride from Clay's suburban home. A mile south of Pompano, beyond the hotels and condos and tucked into a semi-secluded cove—so he's heard—is the nude beach. The beach itself doesn't have a name; it's just *nude*. This according to Clay's PE partner, Nina. Nina can sprint like a panther, do fifty chin-ups, and understands how to high-jump. She's on the volleyball team and is a murderous spiker. Clay, at least a head shorter, has adopted a habit of standing on his toes when he is near her. His arches often ache.

Yesterday, between sit-ups in the gymnasium, Nina told Clay that Ms. Flagrant, the PE teacher, went to the nude beach on weekends. "It's why you don't see tan lines around her bra strap," Nina casually explained. Though Clay spent all of warm-up time—particularly when Ms. Flagrant participated in toe-touches—staring at what the bra contained, he nearly never considered the strap lines.

"Nude beach?" he'd said, winded.

"Yup. It's close. You can see *everything*. Even her mons venus."

Clay had no idea what Nina was talking about. Dad, who did the Puberty Talk one recent awkward weekend, never said squat about Mom's planets—Venus or otherwise. And, quite frankly, he doesn't want to think about Mom's anything. "Really?" he'd said.

"Yup," Nina replied, nodding her head. She kept her hair in a tight coil and never let it down during school. "I'll draw you a map. See for yourself."

Clay is adept at zoning out. Ordinarily, when an adult is prat-
tling on about this or that, his mouth parts slightly and his eyelids
dip. Though he'll know soon enough, he has no idea how much information his brain is sponging despite his lack of attention. Meaning: he doesn't know what he knows. Which is why he wasn't really
paying attention to the Puberty Talk or the mandatory sex ed class (in
which he received a C-). He is, he's sure, a few beats behind his ninth-
grade peers in the sexual experience category. Nina drew the map on
a brown paper towel. Her looping penmanship seemed salacious and
filled with promise. Where the shore bends there's a boldly drawn X.
"That's where you'll find the booty," she joked.

Though he laughed then, he's not laughing now. His tongue is
protruding slightly from chapped lips and he is gripping the map in a
hand that is also wrapped around the bike's curved handlebar. Clay is
wearing his favorite tank top which has the word *Thrash* emblazoned
in black upon the yellow-colored cotton shirt front. His freckled shoulders are shades lighter than his arms. He's wearing his green bathing
suit. There's a striped towel draped around his neck and his sunglasses
keep slipping down the bridge of his hastily sun-screened nose. He's
two blocks away from his house before it occurs to him that he might
have to get nude in order to gain access to the nude beach. Like, maybe
there's a naked security guard holding a menacing billy club who will
deny him access unless he strips down. This possibility causes him to
swerve off the sidewalk and nearly into the street.

A few months ago, Clay's mother took him to the doctor for a
physical. He didn't want her to enter the exam room with him, but
once upon a time there was an incident, so unless you were eighteen you had to be accompanied by an adult. Doc, who knew the
Crenshaws, made corny jokes about the solar system and flirted with
Clay's mother, whom he called Ms. Galaxy. Lots of men acted gaga
around her. "It's the red hair," she explained to Clay one afternoon

once the UPS guy finally drove away. "You'll see." To that, Clay had said, "Oh." To the doctor, during the physical, he had asked, "How tall am I going to get?"

"That depends on your genes. How tall is his progenitor?" the doc asked Mom.

"Not very," she said with a contorted half-snort.

"Ha ha," the doctor said, standing up straight and twirling his stethoscope.

Clay's inquiry about his height was a decoy. A setup for what he really wanted to ask, which was: "How big will my member get?" After cycling through an online thesaurus, surprised at how many words there were for penis—cock, chub, peter, putz, tool, johnson, prick, lizard, willy—he'd settled on *member*, a word he felt someone might use in a doctor's office during a physical. He didn't, however, have the balls—the gonads, stones, nuts, rocks, testes, family jewels—to inquire in the presence of his mother. And he didn't know how to get her to leave. So he slung his head low on the paper-wrapped examining table, surrounded by herpes posters and glass containers filled with tongue depressors, and kept his trap shut. He coughed lightly when asked.

Clay suspects his member isn't the proper, healthy, normal size for a boy his age. The only porn he's been able to view through the internet filter on his computer features girls. Jeff's laptop doesn't have filters, and though his *ex*-friend invited Clay over to check out some *hardcore shit*, Clay wasn't comfortable with that plan one iota. Sitting with Jeff in the filthy small bedroom with the squeaky overhead fan and Jeff's musky body odor circulating all over the place while gawking at people fucking and then maybe checking out the guy's schlong—and *schlong* seems like the word they'd use in the porn industry—struck Clay as highly problematic. Like, what if he became aroused? How does the brain and body work in concert when his vision moves from the exposed parts of the woman to the exposed parts of the man to Jeff grinning like a lunatic and breathing heavy? Where does the eroticism begin and where does it end? Might wires get crossed, circuits shorted? Plus, those porn guys' wieners are probably not proportional to the general male population. Likely they had to try out for the part. On top of all that, sometimes Clay receives spam in his email account promoting penis pumps, a concept that baffles him. So, yeah; forget about getting naked on the nude beach with his possibly-still-developing manhood in front of Ms. Flagrant.

When Clay decides to turn around, the loose shoelace on his left Reebok catches in the teeth of the bike chain and causes him to wobble, distracted, into the street.

One thing drivers in South Florida refuse to do is stop at stop signs. The green F-five million Ford Super-Drive Mega-Powered quadruple-duallied—you could hardly call it a pickup truck, more like pickup *tank*—collides with the agitated boy on the bike as he's attempting to cross Riverside Drive. Clay and his ten-speed pinwheel into the sky. Suspended in that millisecond, it's kind of a cool thrill. He's *flying*! Maybe it's actually not cool for a millisecond; more like a nanosecond? Or less, even. Half-heartbeat? Clay's not sure. Though he's been taught it, the boy is not considering Newton's laws of motion. Force (f) = mass (m) times acceleration (a). If he remembered that every action has an equal and opposite reaction he would never think that careening through the air is cool, no matter the brief, nearly incomprehensible time he spends soaring.

The boy awkwardly reacquaints himself with the earth. His apple-colored hair reddens from the split-skull seepage.

———

How was Nina to know that her little white lie re: the nude beach whereupon the resplendently buxomed Ms. Flagrant sprawled in the buff would lead to such ill-fated consequences? You cannot rightly blame her. She wasn't the hit-and-run driver. She didn't twist his arm or hold a gun to his head. In fact, Nina tells herself as she does partner-less sit-ups in the gymnasium during PE, she was, if you think about it, extending Clay—an awkward boy by anyone's account—a favor. Unlike the other freshman, who are absolutely *distraught* by the news Clayton Crenshaw has slipped into a coma out of which he may or may not awaken, unlike *them*, she actually talked with him. Kind of even maybe liked him. He'd sometimes slip into a faraway stare when they were in art class that enshrouded him with what you might call an air of contemplative mystery. She'd heard that his mother "read the stars," so he was bound to be at least a little deepdish. Probably he saw constellations when he gazed into the night sky.

Now, of course, since three weeks have passed and flowers have been sent on behalf of the school, fewer and fewer students are thinking about their classmate. Summer is on the horizon and the young know better than to grieve for long.

Still, though, Nina hasn't forgotten. She nearly spilled the beans to her friend Amy the other day during volleyball practice. Almost admitted that she told Clay about the nonexistent nude beach. But, so; no, she didn't. Bit her tongue instead. The tip of which—her tongue—is protruding from her lips as she does solo sit-ups on the sweat-funky old gym mats. She wonders, since she knows she's not going to say anything to her friend, if there's something she can do. To help Clay. Or, at least, to make herself feel better about her microscopic (maybe even smaller) role in the unfortunate incident. Wonders so hard she loses track of the number of sit-ups she is completing.

Life, Nina knows, is a series of hurdles. Or hoops. Hurdles or hoops over or through which she must jump. See an obstacle, address it, and conquer it. Just because you ignore a problem doesn't mean the problem ignores you. It can fester. It—a nagging sense of guilt—has been gnashing her guts since she heard about the accident. There, now; at least she can admit it to herself. Acknowledge an itsy-bitsy crumb of responsibility. She did draw him the map. He was on the way to the beach. He is in a coma. These are facts. Maybe she's at one hundred and twenty sit-ups by now.

What you're supposed to do when you are able to admit you've done something wrong is do something right. You counter-activate. Detangle. Turn the tide. Once you've jumped over/through the hurdle/hoop you feel better. Move forward. It's scientific.

"Hey," Ms. Flagrant says. "Wake up, Nina. That's enough."

And there it is. There *they* are. Ms. Flagrant is leaning down, hands lightly resting atop Nina's bony knees, her T-shirt drooping low enough for Nina to plainly see two ample melons tucked tightly into her teacher's fashionable black sports bra.

"Ah," Nina says, eyes full, "right." The pinprick of a pre-idea scuttles up the downy hair upon the back of her neck.

Ms. Flagrant is also Coach Flagrant. She's in charge of the girls' volleyball team. Nina, with Amy and her other teammates, stays after school for practice every Monday, Wednesday, and Friday. Since she only lives a block away and her parents work until 5:30, Nina catches a ride home with Amy's older brother Flint, a senior, who stays after for band.

Today is Friday. PE was on Wednesday. Nina's had two days to come up with a plan. Now, as she and Amy wait atop the hood of Flint's yellow Mitsubishi Mirage, it's time to execute it.

"Oh shit," Nina says, "I forgot my algebra book. We've got that test on Monday. I'm going to run and get it."

Amy is texting, which is what she always does. "You can borrow mine," she says, eyes down.

"No. I've got notes in the margins. It'll just take a sec."

"Hurry," Amy mutters. "Flint won't wait."

"I will," Nina says, already moving toward the entrance.

The gym is located in the left wing of the school. She speed-walks toward the girls' locker room where she purposefully left her textbook beneath a bench.

Coach Flagrant always showers at the school on Fridays, after the girls have gone. Fridays, she joins Ms. Roarback, Ms. Jentworth, and Ms. Kashari for happy hour at Ballyhoo's and it's just easier for her to go directly from school.

The plan is simple: snap a shot of Ms. Flagrant in the buff, print out a copy (her father has a color printer in his office), fold it up, and send it anonymously to Clay at the hospital (without a return address). Won't he be surprised when he wakes up? Beats daffodils and saccharine drivel inked into a Hallmark card.

Within Nina there is a space occupying an unchartered region of the occipital lobe—a place that doesn't translate reason in a way that's recognizable to neuroscientists—where, deep down, she believes that the photograph might actually compel Clay to open his eyes. Like, somehow, he's waiting for Nina to complete his unfinished quest. Clay is the damsel in distress and Nina the chivalrous knight. Ms. Flagrant is like the golden chalice or fleece or whatever. She can't remember exactly what King Arthur and the other fools were searching for. The point is, a picture is worth a thousand words and maybe a nude one is worth more.

Nina closes the locker room door quietly. She withdraws her cellphone and arms the camera. There is the hollow splatter of water slapping tile in the shower arena. The school used to provide curtains in two stall sections for the shy girls, but the plastic became moldy, the janitor removed them, and they haven't been replaced. Flattening herself against the outside wall, Nina cranes her head—ninja style—to see what she can see. Sure enough, there's Ms. Flagrant all lathered, back turned, humming a tune Nina can't quite place. Nina zooms in and waits for Coach to turn around so she can capture all of the goods. Flagrant bends to fetch the shampoo. She works it in like a pro, humming as she kneads. Finally, she spins. Nina snaps rapid-fire shots—click, click, click—like the paparazzi. Her heart whiplashes. Palms sweat. The tiny hairs on the nape of her neck bristle a warning that she needs to bolt, like *now*. Carefully, Nina retreats. She snags the algebra book, squeezes out the door, sprints down the hall, bursts outside, and jogs to the parking lot where Amy and Flint are waiting.

Later, after dinner, in the privacy of her locked bedroom, sitting at her desk, Nina reviews the pictures. In the first shot, there's so much steam that Ms. Flagrant's body appears wavy. In the second shot, Coach's eyes are half open as she's swiping away shampoo and she sort of resembles a zombie. Either Nina's holding the cellphone crooked or Ms. Flagrant's boobs are uneven because they're lopsided in the next shot. She's kind of squatting, for some reason, in this one. She needs to shave her legs. In the last shot her lips, mid-hum, are puckered and blubbering. She looks as erotic as a sea turtle. The pictures wouldn't rouse a horndog from a catnap, let alone a sensitive boy in a full-blown coma. Plus, and, well, yeah—she should have thought of this earlier—Ms. Flagrant is in the shower not at the beach. Clay's quest was to the mythical shore. So this won't work at all. She punches delete. Then "Tomorrow" hits her. The ditty from *Annie*. That's the tune Coach was humming. Nina can't quell a pinch of embarrassment she feels for her teacher. It's the kind of kids' show tune she might have whistled when she was like eight or something. She half thinks, as she lets her hair down for bed, that she should spill the beans to Amy so they can both enjoy a hearty chuckle at the expense of their teacher. Course, how will she explain overhearing

Flagrant in the shower? The question might arouse suspicion. Then Amy would call Nina a creepster. Or a lesbian. Probably best to stay tight-lipped and come up with another plan.

Bet your bottom dollar that tomorrow there'll be sun.

————

Fucking scientists, man. Fucking *scientists*.

Hello?

Remember what they did to Ming?

Um. Where am I?

They killed him.

I'm dead?

Not you. Ming. Remember?

What happened to me?

It's boring. You got plowed. Now you're in a coma, blah, blah, blah. You need to pay better attention.

Coma?

Yeah. And you're not alone.

Are you God?

Don't be a moron. I'm you, you're me; we're we.

You're like, my spirit?

Neurologists would say I am a series of cognitive synapses firing. When your blood pressure drops like it's doing now, the vagus nerve delivers blood from the heart to the semiconscious territory in your cerebellum.

So, I'm dreaming?

Not technically. If you were asleep, you'd wake up when your body was done resting. When your blood had enough oxygen. The stasis you're in doesn't operate like that.

Why not?

Excessive brain churn. Overstimulation. Unfinished thoughts have breached the floodgates. Questions are rising from the depth and waiting.

For answers?

Yes.

I want to know when I'll wake up.

I already told you that you're not asleep. Plus, a better question would be *if* you'll regain consciousness, not when.

Will I?

Hard to say. That's what the doctors told your parents when they asked.

They're here?

Mom's nearby.

Where?

Listen, you're getting agitated. Let's slow down. We'll return to Ming in a minute. What do you last remember?

I was on my bike. Heading to the nude beach. My shoelace came undone.

Good.

Then what?

Then now. Here, with me. See if you can delve deeper.

Into the past?

When you were a kid, you used to wonder where the Tooth Fairy took the teeth.

And *why* she took them.

But now you know Mom keeps them in her jewelry box. She's going to superglue them to a frame with a picture of you as a baby. The one where you're at the beach.

Pail on my head. Clutching sand. Naked but for the soggy diaper.

That's the one. Grinning slack jaw. A pre-teeth snapshot.

All right. That's cool if it'll make her happy. Now what?

You ready for Ming?

The clam?

Born during the Ming dynasty.

I remember. The online headline was something like, "Scientists accidently kill oldest living animal."

Oldest *known* living animal. There's a difference. In order to determine an official age, the clam had to be pried open. You have to count the rings. Scientists were too forceful.

It died because scientists were curious about its age.

That's what the article said. Five hundred and nine years old. You found the news ironic. And then you wondered what the *new* oldest known living animal is, but instead of looking that up…

I visited Hott Girlz Xposed.

Correct.

Still don't know how that site gets through the internet filter…

…now that Ming is dead, Shakes is the oldest known living animal.

Another clam?

Quahog. An *Arctica islandica*. Dredged off Newfoundland. He's four hundred and twelve years old. Named after Shakespeare.

Who cares?

Everyone should. You, in particular.

Why?

You know.

I do?

Yeah. Everything is in your head.

How do I get it out?

Coax it. Bit by bit. Think it through. People want to live forever, right? These quahogs are capable of living for hundreds of years. If we can figure out how they are able to live so long, maybe we can extend our own lives.

All right. That makes sense. So, how are they able to live so long?

Scientists believe it's their slow metabolism, but that's not the reason. The reason, I'm afraid, doesn't make sense.

It's not reasonable.

True, all the same, though. And important.

Tell me.

You ready?

I am.

Clams live off the dreams of children.

They do what?

They've got these infinitely long microscopic tongues—invisible to humans—that shoot out of their mouth and probe the dreamscape. They can sense innocence and when they find it, always in the young, they bore into the ear canals and probe kid skulls. They gorge on pure thoughts, suck away guiltlessness, then recoil, sated, and clamp that goodness shut tight where they nest in the muck.

Um. They're like aliens?

That's why adults are such puny, frightened husks. They've been siphoned by ancient clams.

That's hard to swallow.

Better wrap your head around it because there's a quahog off Pompano Beach who has a taste for you right now. Ponce de Leon sailed over her, back in the day.

Really?

Can't you feel it?

Well. I mean. My toes tingle a little.

That's it. Wiggle those fuckers.

———

It takes the entire weekend for Nina to work out the specifics of her next attempt at leaping the hurdle and/or diving through the hoop in terms of procuring a nude photo and awakening Clay from his maybe-permanent slumber. Plan B isn't as simple as Plan A. It requires great sacrifice on Nina's part, which she has convinced herself she's willing to offer.

Recently, Amy bought her brother Flint a retractable selfie stick for his eighteenth birthday. What you do is slide your cellphone into a mechanical claw, telescope the pole, and trigger the shot. Or you can use a timer. It allows you to take full body shots, not just close-ups. Flint uses it when he plays guitar.

Monday, after practice, when Flint drops the girls off at Amy's house (before driving to the mall where he works at Music and More), Nina says she needs to use the bathroom. It can't wait until she walks home. Amy doesn't care. She slumps upon the caramel-colored horsehair sofa and texts Jeff Andrews, her on-again/off-again maybe boyfriend.

Amy lives in a single-story house which resembles all the other homes in the neighborhood. Once every few years a hurricane will salsa across South Florida. It'll huff and puff and blow shit down. The closer a building squats to the ground, the shorter it falls when a big bad storm strikes. There are pictures of sailboats adorning the walls. The floors are covered with off-white Spanish tiles which emit a timid squeal as Nina tiptoes down the hall.

Flint's bedroom is across from the bathroom. Casting a furtive glance over her shoulder to make sure Amy isn't looking, Nina sneaks into the room.

Nina has been in the bedroom before. Sometimes Flint will force Nina and Amy to sit on the unmade bed and listen to him play original songs on his acoustic guitar. What he used to do was demand that someone film him so he could upload the tune on MyRiffs and wait to be discovered. Now, with the selfie stick, he can do it himself.

Flint's got an aquarium next to his bed in which a pale-colored iguana named Rump—short for Rumpelstiltskin—dozes under a heat lamp. One of the recent topics of discussion at the Buckner residence is what's going to happen to Rump once Flint moves to college in the fall. The parents have already said no way are they taking care of it. Amy has flat-out refused. The thing freaks her out with its perpetually molting tail and the creepy sound of its reptilian nails scratching at the newspaper-lined metal pan at the bottom of the cage. The sound, she claims, makes her teeth vibrate. Plus, its excrement reminds her of guacamole, which is one of her favorite foods. So, if her parents try to make her watch Rump, she's threatened to set it free. South Floridians love to purchase exotic reptiles, keep them for a while, and then release them into the wild where they can fuck shit up. All Flint is asking is for someone to like babysit Rump while he's in Gainesville. Dorms don't allow pets. The average captive iguana can live for fifteen years with proper care. Rump's only three. When Flint approached Nina about it—he'd pay her to take care of it—she said maybe.

If you look at it from a certain angle Rump resembles a little prince. Nina has wondered how long she could force it to wear a purple satin cape if she looped it around the neck.

Now, standing in the heat-lamp light, Nina doesn't have time to consider the lizard. She has to stay focused on the plan and not wonder about the source of the stink in the room. It's like foreign cheese or perhaps goat milk. But that's not the point. She's here to locate the selfie stick. To *borrow* it, without asking, and return it before Flint realizes it's gone.

The selfie stick is not next to the cluttered computer desk or leaning against a rickety faux-wood bookshelf. Dropping to her knees, Nina lifts the comforter and peers under the bed. No stick. There is a beach towel partially draped over a shoebox. Curious, she stretches her long arms and tugs the box to her. Inside, curled to conform to the shape of the container, is an array of *Bazoombas* magazines. Unable to resist, Nina flips one open. The girls assume a number of unnatural poses as they stand near a variety of props: a blonde straddles a saw-horse, a patriotic brunette is clutching a pole and waving an American flag, a cheerleader is bending low to fetch her pompoms. All of the women are healthily endowed up top and practically bare below. For the most part, their lipsticked mouths are puckered, glistening, and partly parted. Though she would like to thumb through a few more, to get some pointers, including the *Exotic Erotic Island* edition, Nina is in a hurry. She crams the magazines back into the box.

The selfie stick is in the closet next to an empty guitar stand. Retracted, it's the size of her forearm. She slides it beneath her shirt, along her spine, and tucks the handle into the back of her volleyball shorts. Then, quietly, she exits the room, slips into the bathroom, flushes the toilet—for good measure—and walks stiffly back into the living room. Amy is twirling her curly hair around her index finger and watching a video on her phone.

"Thanks," Nina says, grabbing her backpack. "See you tomor-row."

After dinner, dishes, homework, some computer time, and the goodnights, Nina closes her bedroom door and slips beneath her sheets, still clothed. Her parents, like clockwork, will read in bed until ten and drift off by ten thirty. Just to be on the safe side, Nina waits until eleven thirty before climbing out of bed, opening her win-dow, removing the screen, and crawling outside. Her room is right next to the air conditioner. It's whirring like an accomplice. When she's on the moist, tough St. Augustine grass, she crouches low and scampers to the front of the house in her flip-flops.

The beach is only a mile away. Nina hurries along the sidewalk. The night is quiet but for a few cars on A1A. This is the second time she has snuck out. The first time, with Amy and a few of Flint's friends, they lit a bonfire, drank beer, and skinny-dipped. Well, Nina didn't get naked—she stayed in her underwear—but the boys did. One kid's bare ass was as pale as the moon. Jiggling and skimming beneath the surface of the water, tousling with his buddies, his butt looked like he was being chased by a flounder. She snickered and sucked down two grape-flavored wine coolers which she paid for in the morning. That was several months ago.

Tonight, the moon is in the sky. The beach is empty. Sand stretches horizontally to a vanishing point. Lights from a Marriott a half mile south appear swollen in the hazy, humidity-drenched air. The lighthouse guarding the Hillsborough inlet is a dizzy Cyclops.

Nina wastes no time stripping down to nothing. She sets her clothes in a neat pile atop her flip-flops. The sand is still warm from the heat of the day. The breeze rolling off the ocean tamps down the sweat she accumulated on the walk here and momentarily prickles the flesh on her arms. She sets her phone to camera mode, clips it to the selfie stick, erects the pole, and loosens the tight bun on her head. Before getting into position, she arranges her hair in a net across her face. It's crucial that her identity is protected. The idea is to send Clay a photograph of a naked girl, not a nude picture of herself. Only the anonymous body matters.

Nina props herself up on an elbow and gazes behind her. She can see the tiny craters where her feet made impact with the sand. Contorting her arm, she triggers a shot. Then another and another. She figures if she takes enough pictures there's bound to be something she can use. The waves ceaselessly break in frothy phosphorescence. She rolls over, lifts her chin high, clicks away. Leans forward a bit then back, arches her legs; sort of somersaults. Does a push-up and a crunch. She dismisses a split. Then she calls it quits. She wipes away sand before dressing.

It's only when she's safely back in her room, wearing her favorite pajamas—with the alternating pink and red hearts—and under the protection of her covers that she dares to look at the pictures. The first photo—delete—has a glare. In the second shot—delete—she can see an animalistic red eye. In the third picture—delete—it looks like she's about to sneeze. She can't believe how obvious her macaroni-shaped birthmark appears on her knee. Delete. Her belly button's got a gallon of sand in it. Delete. When she's lifting into a backbend she resembles a wobbly-kneed giraffe calf trying to find its feet. Delete. In the last shot there's a green glow covering her two-by-four body and the glint reflecting off her teeth behind her scraggly hair makes her appear hungry. She looks more like an emaciated sea hag than a perky mermaid. Delete, delete, delete.

Nina throws the phone across the room, repulsed. She's never hated herself as much as she does at this moment. The offending selfie stick propped against her dresser enrages. She has half a mind to leap from the bed and smash it over her knee. Or use it to bash out someone's brains. Or electrify it and shove it up Clay's ass. Wake him right up.

These things, of course, she cannot do. She curls into a ball and cocoons beneath the floral-patterned sheets. She can't destroy Flint's selfie stick. It needs to be returned to that dank room with the stinky iguana and the never-made bed. Oh, and what's under the bed. Those farfetched women. Missile-titted cartoons. If that's what boys want, fuck 'em. Swearing, even if it's only in her head, sort of helps. Rocking back and forth slightly calms. Nina begins to simmer. Heart rate returns to normal. Breathing evens. She wonders what Clay's thinking about. Boobs, probably. So easy to come by. Always right in front of her.

Like everyone else, Nina has heard the advice about counting sheep as a means of falling asleep. So, she begins: one, two, three. Then she imagines a tiny version of herself jumping over the sheep as they approach. Four, five, six. The numbers rapidly advance. At two hundred and thirty-nine, the sheep morph into clouds and instead of hurdling them the mini-Nina in her brain dives through. Cloud by cloud she leaps and counts; leaps and counts. Then, right where the fibers of a dream meet consciousness, Nina discovers Plan C.

———

Except for brief sorties home to refresh, Vivian has remained seated next to her son in the small hospital room ever since Clay slipped into his coma. Today marks one month.

In the beginning, a wave of well-wishers sent sympathy cards and flowers. Viv's sister Lilly has visited twice. Clay's father comes every other week. He never stays long since he refuses to sit down and really detests looming over his boy trying to will him back to the land of the living. He enters the room, kisses Clay's furrowed brow, hovers with his back to his ex-wife, leaning on his heels, listens to the whoosh and tick of the ventilators, kisses him again on the forehead, whispers something private, and leaves.

Viv nests in the navy-blue chair with the anemic seat cushion. She's slight enough to contract her entire body so that it fits in the tired piece of furniture. She's brought a baby blanket her mother—Clay's deceased grandmother—crocheted, which she huddles beneath. Her unkempt cabernet-colored hair has been swept into a punishing ponytail. The hair is so tight it forces her eyes into unblinking walnut-colored slits. Her vision is ever so slightly blurry. From her hunched vantage, beneath the only window in the room (which overlooks a sun-bedazzling parking lot), she can see the starboard side of the bed and the mostly unblemished portion of Clay's face. Each week doctors remove a little more of his bandages. He's gradually transitioning from mummy back to boy.

The flowers from a bouquet sitting upon the nightstand are in various stages of decay. The principal of Pompano High School sent a sizeable glass vase brimming with lilacs, violets, and forget-me-nots. A number of students signed the Get Well Soon card. Stench from the old water clogged with putrefying deadheads rises into the air conditioning zephyrs. The sweetly briny scent blows over the boy at exact intervals (every forty-five minutes) and for precisely the same amount of time (eight minutes). It's always seventy-two degrees in the hospital. When Clay inhales the scent into his perfectly functioning nasal cavities, the good old olfactory gives a swift kick to the hypothalamus, which triggers the quasi-memory/invention of a shadowself or imaginary friend of sorts, an evolutionary micro-ego pinched in the saline of the brain. It's an echo still reverberating from our single-cell squirming-from-primordial-ooze days.

"Good afternoon, Ms. Crenshaw," Nurse Goldwin says, entering the hospital room. "And how are we today?" Two of Nurse Goldwin's greatest features are her top front teeth. They are whiter than bleached bone. For this reason, she almost always smiles. And she keeps her face super tan to enhance the contrast.

"I'm good," Viv says, moving from a fetal to an upright position in the chair. She absentmindedly folds the baby blanket.

"Your boy got mail!" Goldwin singsongs. She holds a greeting-card-sized envelope up just beneath her chin so it's impossible to avoid those brilliant chompers. "Want me to set it on the nightstand?"

"No. I'll take it."

"There isn't a return address. And there's a note on the back which reads, *For Clay Crenshaw's eyes only.* Isn't that strange? Maybe your boy has a secret ad-mi-r-er!" The nurse does a little shimmy-shake, holding the envelope and wagging her head to and fro.

"Thanks," Viv says when the nurse finally hands it over. She sets the envelope in her lap and contemplates slinking back into the chair.

The position isn't comfortable and Viv likes it that way. She's not here to sleep. Her lower back aches, the wooden arms of the chair leave unsightly indentions in her calves, her shoulder blades bend, and a cinched nerve in her neck gives her a perpetual low-grade headache. Since she cannot risk curling up and spooning Clay—she's been reprimanded for doing this and warned about the dangers of tangling ventilation tubes—all that's really left to do is linger in mild discomfort nearby. To wait. Then wait. Wait.

"Aren't you going to open that?"

"What?"

"The card. You're not going to wait until he opens his eyes, are you?"

"No. I'm not. Going to wait, I mean."

Viv tears the top of the envelope with fingernails flecked with maroon polish. Inside is a white, off-brand greeting card with the words *I'm Sorry* scripted in a carefree font meant to communicate a breezy, light, *Hey, it's not so hard to forgive, is it?* style. When Viv opens the card, a folded piece of something drops into her lap. Before investigating, she reads the handwritten note neatly penned in black ink on the inside of the flap: *Is this what you're looking for?* The card is unsigned.

"What is that?" Goldwin asks.

The magazine page in Viv's lap has been folded four times. Each time she unfolds a flap, the photograph of the naked woman becomes more complete, until, finally, both Viv and Goldwin—who has sidled next to the chair—can see the improbably chested and dark-haired model propped upon an elbow inside an enormous clam. The picture is ripped along the edges as if torn hastily out of a nudie magazine which resides under the bed of a high school senior with a sickly iguana by a young girl surreptitiously returning a selfie stick and resorting to Plan C: send Clay a nude shot from the *Exotic Erotic Island* issue of *Bazoombas* magazine.

"Is this some kind of prank?" Goldwin asks.

Viv isn't sure. It might be. Or maybe not. Her mind is mired in a grief-stricken molasses.

The woman in the photograph has gray-green eyes the exact shade of the cloudless sky. There's a placid sea in the background. Around her neck is a gaudy string of pearls. Though it's impossible to tell from the photo, this is the first time Mindy, the model, has been to Greece and the first time she has posed inside an enormous clam. The photographer wanted to pay homage to Botticelli's *The Birth of Venus*. The shell is made of a hard plastic and hurts the elbow upon which Mindy is leaning. She is battling back the pain, sucking in her stomach, and attempting to keep her lips lifted slightly in a way that resembles Venus in the painting. The photographer, who majored in Art History, kept insisting that her mouth must appear as if she is hiding a secret from the onlooker. "Don't you have any secrets?" he'd asked. Though she did, she couldn't figure out how her face was supposed to suggest them. They called it quits after two hours and went with a shot that, according to the photographer, makes Mindy seem distressed. Not that it much matters. Most people who subscribe to *Bazoombas* don't do so for the artistic allusions. They don't spend a lot of time gawking at faces. Instead, eyes dart to the bountiful chest, the curve of hips, and the mile-long sculpted legs. Viv, though, traces the landscape of the body to Mindy's feet. When she is not posing as a Greek goddess upon the tar-spotted sandy shoreline of the Mediterranean Sea, Mindy is a waitress at a seafood restaurant in Toledo, Ohio. She's been scuttling from the kitchen to the tables in pumps for years, since she was fourteen. As a result, she has bunions. Squeezing into heels is torture. And though this isn't a characteristic she knows she possesses, when she situates one foot atop the other, in profile, the jut from the protruding bone at the base of the big toes creates a space between her feet in the shape of an elongated heart.

It's there, in the photograph. Viv spots it right away and thinks, *How curious*. This is the first thought she has had in the last month that didn't revolve around Clay.

The flame-orange painted tips of the model's toenails are angling toward the sea. In fact, Mindy's entire body is sort of shaped like an arrow. She is a needle within the compass of the clam. Though this, too, is impossible to know since it's not in the photo, she is pointing the viewer toward a great mystery. She is unwittingly directing you to a fantastic treasure beyond the limitations of the glossy page. All you have to do is walk in a straight line from those posed toes. Crunch the sand and wade into the bathwater-warm shallows. Then swim. Breaststroke for two miles. You can do it. Never mind the waves. All right. Now stop. Catch your breath. Doggy paddle. Inhale. Take in a boatload of oxygen. Then, ready or not, dive. Swim straight down. Further. Deeper. Keep eyes peeled. See that faint light? The eerie blue glow? Good. Hang there, suspended in the water, cheeks puffed, hair rising. Look at what you've found.

The dark water resembles the night sky and bursting from the gloom appears a galaxy. In front of you a wash of countless stars swirl around a bright epicenter. Get closer. What you've discovered is alive. Not a star, an animal. The corkscrew of celestial neon pinpricks are actually luminescent tendrils trailing a translucent orb. It's *Turritopsis dohrnii*. The immortal jellyfish. Its bioluminescence creates light to attract prey. Scientists call this jellyfish immortal because it doesn't appear to die. Its cells don't age, they regenerate. They transdifferentiate. The jellyfish essentially recycles itself, morphing from an immature polyp to an adult then back to the polyp and so on and so forth forever and ever. Don't ask how. The answer will give you the bends. Just squint at it. The spectral radiance reminds you of a ghost. The hypnotic undulation is moving in rhythm to your pulse. See the red bloom inside the bell-shaped gelatinous body? Though it looks like a heart, it's the stomach. Though you want to reach in and grab the vibrating mass, return to shore, and thrust it into the space left by the model's feet—you're sure it's a perfect match—resist the urge. Just because it's immortal doesn't mean it can't die.

Besides, you don't have the luxury of time. You have to make a decision: rise to the surface or sink into the unfathomable lurking dark. It's up to you. We're all waiting.

EVERY HEAVY THING

I'M LYING ON YOUR old bath towel upon the beach getting a tan and thinking about you—an open book in my lap—when a lizard drops from the sky and lands on my bare chest. This is where we used to go, back when we were we; a quiet cove away from both tourists and locals alike. You wondered why nobody came here but I didn't. I wondered why you bothered to wonder rather than just enjoying what we'd stumbled upon: golden sand, ripe sun, frolicking waves, and us alone together.

We know why now, don't we? The story. The legend a passing fisherman explained to us one morning. You only half heard him because he creeped you out with his alligator teeth and astronaut eyes. I listened. In the story, an *unwell* woman attempted to drown herself in the shallows just offshore. Lugged her backpack filled with every heavy thing she could scrounge from her apartment—a toaster, paperweights, iron, silverware, five porcelain birds painted various shades of indigo—and trudged into the surf. Apparently she used to dance. You might say she had a gift. She was engaged to a man who cheated on her—an oh-so-familiar tune, right? He did the infidelity mambo. When he called off the engagement, she decided to call off her life. But she didn't drown. Kept her arms in the straps for as long as possible, willing herself to hold on until the end. Couldn't, though. The body doesn't always obey the brain. Eventually she let go. Rose to the surface. Floated a while. Caught her breath. Then she dove back down to the backpack to fetch one other heavy thing. Swam ashore. Blew her brains out. Right here on our private sandy stretch of beach. Fisherman said, and you scoffed at this, that every few days or so the figure of a woman appears in the sand. A sandwoman. Said he'd seen it with his own eyes. The details are too clear for it to have been molded with a human hand, he claimed. Sand stained red in a bloom around her head. Got her arms folded over her chest like arms in a coffin. Or like she's still trying to clutch that backpack. Or maybe, and this is what the fisherman said he believed, she's trying to dig a hole into her chest and grab her sandy heart so she can rise up and fling it into the sea.

I can't tell if the lizard is dead. Might be. It doesn't weigh much. Though it rises and falls when I breathe, I'd have to stop breathing to determine if it could go it alone. The eyes are pinched-shut slits. He could be stunned or faking. I don't know. I don't even know where it came from. Nothing above but ribbons of cloud. It's one of those commonplace anoles capable of changing color from brown to green. Just an everyday creature I'd ordinarily overlook.

Do you remember the lizard story I told you? Back before we moved into our apartment? You were sad because you'd flattened one with your bicycle. You'd been biking along the sidewalk when it scuttled out in front of you and froze. When you swerved, it swerved, too. You said you could feel the tremor, all the way up in your handlebars, from its fragile bones popping. That seemed unlikely to me. What you felt was guilt. I did the *There-there-theres*. Talked reason. Explained how tetrapods have miniscule brains. They don't think like us. Like me. Then, as an example, I told you about my first experience with a lizard.

My parents moved us down to Florida—the kickstand of the country—when I was seven. There are no lizards where I was born.

Back then I was intimidated by the way the red flap on a lizard's throat puffs out when he sees you, though it's just his way of trying to seem more dangerous than he is. On a balmy afternoon I decided I was going to catch one. I'd seen a teenager by the pool snag an anole by wiggling the fingers in his left hand as a distraction and then snatching with his right. Like the way you kill a fly. I tried the technique with a chameleon peeking from some palm fronds. My first swipe at it was tentative. Though I told myself I wasn't afraid, that was a lie. My hands were ready but my brain had reservations. What if it bit me? Were these things venomous?

As it turns out, it didn't matter. When I half-heartedly tried to snatch the thing, he dropped into the cranky grass and dashed straight into an air conditioning unit. The machine wasn't running. I remember standing there, a few paces away, hoping it would be safe inside. It wasn't. In Florida, there's no rest for an air conditioner. Within seconds it grumbled alive. Then, before I had a chance to flinch, the lizard flew out of the unit, smacked me right in the chest, and fell to my feet. I stood there, stunned, trying to process what had happened. It took my eyes a few heartbeats to realize the little guy wasn't arranged quite right. His bullet-shaped head was angled at ninety degrees. Still, he wasn't all-the-way decapitated. I ran inside, found some Scotch tape, and hustled back. Back then I didn't know the difference between repairable and irreparable.

In hindsight, I shouldn't have told you that story. It's just that you were so upset about the bone-popping bicycle incident. When I first started telling you, I thought I might be able to make it sound funny. I mean, it's pretty pathetic, right? Me to the rescue with my transparent tape! You know how characters in cartoons try to stick their finger into a hole in a dam to keep it from busting but the fissures keep multiplying and soon the hapless fool runs out of digits and the dam explodes and everything washes away downstream?

That's how I wanted you to see me. Somehow, though, I got off course. My laughter was shrill and ill-timed. When you asked, *What happened next?* I should have lied and said that, when I arrived on the scene—my hero's cape flapping in the wind—the lizard was gone. It wasn't hurt, after all. The light was playing a trick. The gashed throat was just his red flap warning me away. You deserved a lie. I wish I never mentioned the industry of those swift fire ants.

This book I'm not reading is *Zen and the Art of Motorcycle Maintenance*. You recommended it but I don't remember why. I've never even been on a motorcycle. The pages keep turning in the ocean breeze and I let them. This way I can pretend I'm making progress. What I have read—several times now—is the brief note you left me. You wrote it on hotel stationery, a place where I've never stayed. Folded over, it makes a fine bookmark.

A funny thing I picked up from the fry cook yesterday—I may have mentioned Frank—is that if you stare at something long enough, you'll eventually see a human face. He was talking about potatoes but he meant anything. Like, look hard at the underside of your arm and watch it morph into a face of sorts. He explained that this is coded in our brains. I was going to mention this after my shift but I got distracted, obviously. And hey, I wanted to tell you—and this is admittedly kind of weird—when I first saw the piece of paper on the kitchen counter, I thought maybe it was a suicide note. Isn't that crazy? For a split second, when I read your note—*It's not working out. I'm leaving. Sorry.*—I thought you meant leaving this world. Like that girl with the backpack. Though, of course, you're nothing like her. Her note was undoubtedly better. She might have written, *My porcelain heart is a purple sparrow. I'm cracked and clipped and can fly no more.* Or maybe she was bitter and simply wrote, *Fuck you, philanderer!* Perhaps she didn't leave a message and just let the blood stain in the sand speak for itself.

The anole on my chest is kind of grinning. Lizards are probably not as narcissistic as us and don't see reptilian faces everywhere. I wonder what he'll think if he opens his eyes. Will he be frightened, grateful, or indifferent?

One time, and I already told you part of this story so bear with me, I was at a birthday party for this kid named Bubby. The mother had one of those helium tanks, the kind that pitches your voice into a squeak when you inhale and when you talk you sound like Mickey Mouse. Bubby and his friend Marco kept filling up balloons—there were like a million—until the birthday boy had a bright idea. He wondered how many balloons it would take to hoist a lizard into the sky. I was eavesdropping on a lawn chair in the corner while they speculated. The cake, as I recall, was awful, and this fact struck me as really unfair. That was the first time I'd had bad cake. Anyway, so, Marco was the best lizard hunter on our block. He caught one cowering beneath the grill cover and, laughing, the boys looped the string around its neck and tied it super tight. Though I know lizards are not like us—you can't hang them the way you can a man—I still didn't like to see such bald cruelty. I stood up and said as much.

That's when you told me to quit telling you the story because it was making you upset. You had a hunch it wouldn't end well. I don't even know how we got on the subject in the first place. Anyway, I did as you asked and bit my tongue. I didn't explain that it takes three balloons all tied together to support an average-sized anole and when those boys let it go—despite my protests—it lifted into the sky, soared over the rooftops, and began rising. I clutched a handful of decorative stones and chased after it. My aim then, as it is now, was poor. The balloons were orange, red, and green in color. The lizard was brown. It floated into the blue, blue sky.

I know if you were here you'd have a theory. How it got here. You might suggest that it was tucked into the landing gear on an airplane departing from Ft. Lauderdale. That's what you would think if you were here because that's where you would've wanted to be. On an airplane, not in the landing gear. Leaving me to be with that time-share guy. The stowaway recklessly scuttled out, couldn't hold on, and plummeted to earth. I am the X that marks the spot.

Since I'm getting everything off my chest here I should confess that you're not the only one with a secret. Something happened recently that I never mentioned because you wouldn't have believed me and honestly I was too tired to try and explain. Late one night about a month ago, when you were away and I couldn't sleep, I decided to jog here, to our beach. I sat and listened to the hush of the waves. A sliver of moon dipped low and the sky was crowded with constellations. There were so many faces in the stars. Then, on my periphery, I saw something move. At first I thought it was a sea turtle or crab tunneling up for a midnight voyage. The disturbance was only a few yards away from where I sat. Then, as I watched, I saw a nest of red-tipped fingers wiggling around. Soon hands surfaced, then bleached-white arms followed by a stringy mop of seaweed hair. When the head breached the hole and I saw her face, my heart nearly stopped. Her gaunt cheekbones were thatched with thin strips of skin, her grainy teeth jutted from rubbery, blackened lips, and unblinking emerald-colored eyes gathered all the light in the night and hurled it at me. I can still feel the weight of her gaze.

She awkwardly clambered to her feet and stood there with her shoulders hunched, head down, and bony arms dangling at her sides. A chunk of her jaw was missing, and when she turned away from me I saw the gaping maw of her ventilated skull. The wind made a reedy whistle when it blew through her tattered dress. I stood up and prepared to bolt. But I didn't run, see? Although every instinct told me to flee, I waited. I gave her a chance to do whatever it is she needed to do. Which was, as it turned out, sway back and forth with the ebb and flow of the tide in a slow dance with the waves. It was dreamy and unreal. Peaceful somehow I can't explain. I kind of rocked back and forth from foot to foot, with her, in a way. For a moment the beach belonged to us. Then she trudged into the shallows and became shadows, mist, and moonlight. I shuffled home to the empty bed. But now I'm back. I put your towel right where I remember her surfacing. She could reach up at any second, clutch me in her arms, and drag me down.

Hey, but guess what, Amanda? The lizard is still alive! Unlike all those others, he survived. He just opened his prehistoric eyes. Now he's bobbing his chin, nodding an affirmation. Telling me he's all right. When he slides off my chest, his sharp nails scratch tiny red lines into my skin. It doesn't hurt. It's nothing permanent. Hell, if you look closely, you can see that they're already fading.

Y'IDIOT

I'VE BEEN HOLED UP in the apartment, waiting for eviction or my ex-girlfriend to return and pick up her things, when the phone rings. She didn't leave much; just imitation jewelry, one bottle of blue and one bottle of red nail polish, a five pound barbell, a chipped coffee mug, and fancy soap in the shape of a seashell. It all fits into the shoebox I shoved beneath the bed.

The ringing is coming from the land line on the kitchen counter, hidden behind a wall of cereal boxes. Not my cell. My cellphone is inoperable after I threw it into the ocean yesterday. The wind was blowing shoreward and I didn't hurl it with a ton of conviction. This morning I woke up with regret. I lugged the waterproof metal detector into the shallows and retrieved the damaged phone. I also discovered eighty-five cents and a toaster. Both the toaster and the cellphone are drying on the windowsill. My plan for today is to wait and see which one works first. I'm hoping it's the toaster. I've got a half-loaf of bread in the freezer.

I'd forgotten we had a land line, to be honest. It was the ex's idea. Her mother doesn't trust technology and will only use something she can plug into a wall. As a show of support, I gave our phone number to my mother, too. I guess the person calling now is a solicitor, the phone company threatening to turn off the phone, a mother, or the ex.

Because I don't have an answering machine, the phone just keeps ringing. It sounds precisely like the telephones from my youth. After a while it's all I can hear.

Probably, the person on the other end is a robot. Some confused android trying to process data. What's an automaton to do when nothing or nobody picks up? Is it possible for a robot to lose its patience? I don't know but I'm prepared to find out.

I pour a bowl of Corn Flakes and sit down at the kitchen counter. I don't have much food or any milk. I believe the flakes are stale but I can't remember what stale tastes like. Without milk, they have an impressive crunch. When I chew, the ringing is muted.

There's a trickle of seawater streaming from the toaster onto the floor. It's forming an impressive puddle. I coiled the electrical cord into a tight bundle, tucked it into one of the toaster slots, and emptied the sand from the crumb catcher. Surely, if I plugged it in now I'd be electrocuted.

What I should do is yank the telephone cord from the jack, scuttle to the beach, and hurl the phone into the drink. Then it won't be a *land* line anymore. The ex would have hated this joke. All my jokes—even the good ones—were met with a scoff and an eye roll. Sometimes she'd scratch my arm with her sharp nails. Eventually, I quit trying to be funny and now I'm not.

After finishing my cereal, I set the spoon down, pick up the receiver, and say hello.

"Y'idiot?" the man on the other end says. The only person who calls me that is Frank, the fry cook at DinerLand. I bus tables there. Rather, I used to bus tables. I didn't quit or anything, but I've missed many shifts. He's probably calling to fire me.

"Hey," I say. "How'd you get this number?"

"Phonebook."

"Really? I'm listed?"

"Yeah. You're the only Rick Brickman in Broward County."

"That's encouraging."

"But you're not the only idiot."

"Goodbye, Frank."

"No, wait. Don't hang up. I need your help, Bricks."

Bricks is the nickname I told him to use in place of Y'idiot. "I'm kind of busy today," I say.

"Listen," Frank says.

The air conditioner is running. The upstairs neighbors are stomping around. They are either dancing or boxing. A car horn blares intermittently. The water dripping from the windowsill to the tile floor makes a soft, pleasing plop.

"You hear that horn?"

"Yeah."

"Look out your window."

Outside there's a white van idling at the curb. Frank's behind the wheel, waving. He's a big man with big hands.

"How do you know where I live?"

"Just get your ass down here. I've got a crisp Benjamin waiting for you if you help me out with a thing."

"An illegal thing?"

"Slightly, but mostly not."

"I don't know."

"I can do a Benjamin *and* a Grant."

"A grand?"

"Grant. A *Grant*. That's one fifty. Not bad for an afternoon of work."

"I'm boycotting money."

"Please," Frank says. "You can do it for free if you'd like."

Standing over the toaster, I can see rust on the metal coil. The lever is crooked. I'm not sure it will depress. I don't have time to test it now. Frank's waiting for an answer. "I guess," I say, grabbing the cellphone. "Let me put my shorts on."

———

On our way to Food Leopard, Frank explains the job.

"You remember Sharma?"

I'm in the passenger seat. The sun is so bright outside I have to pinch back tears. I used to own sunglasses. The clock in the dash reads 12:34. That's my second favorite time. The van smells like home fries and soggy paper. On Monday, Wednesday, and Friday, before he arrives at DinerLand, Frank delivers newspapers to Blue Zephyrs, the retirement village. I'm not sure how big a village can be before you call it a town, but Blue Zephyrs is huge. It's like a retirement city. I read online somewhere that life expectancy is on the rise and this poses a problem. The Earth can only handle so much of our kind.

Frank has to get up at like four in the morning. Sometimes I go to bed then. He must be asleep before the sun has set. The ex was a morning person, like Frank. She was also a jogger. I don't run unless I'm being chased. Anyway, I didn't think people read papers anymore.

"Old people do," he said when I mentioned this to him a month ago. "For the obits."

"Oh," I'd said.

"You don't know what obits are, do you?"

"I thought you said orbits. For the *orbits*."

"Why would I say orbits? That doesn't make sense."

"Right," I'd said.

"No, Y'idiot. Obits are obituaries. It's where they list dead people. The elderly are friends with a lot of the deceased."

That comment didn't make sense to me. He meant old people's friends die often. Once they're dead, they're no longer friends. They're *ex*-friends you mourn and then forget or occasionally remember. At the time, I didn't correct Frank. The conversation took place before my ex-girlfriend was an ex. Back then she encouraged me to think before speaking so I could avoid saying stupid things.

Now Frank's talking about Sharma. She supplies eggs to the diner. "You guys had a thing," I say.

"*Have* a thing. We still have it. She's the regional manager for Cluck-Cluck Incorporated. They're the fourth largest egg company in Florida. Recently, there's been a salmonella outbreak. I don't suppose you've been watching the news."

"I lost my remote."

"Nine counties have reported incidents. The bad eggs have been traced back to one of Cluck-Cluck's farms. Now Cluck-Cluck's fucked."

"How long have you been waiting to say that?"

"Popped into my head this morning."

"Well, there it is."

"There's been a major recall. The FDA inspected the farm and found rats and roaches crawling everywhere. Nasty shit. Everything shut down. Corporate is buying back all the eggs in an effort to avoid lawsuits. Customers are getting fully refunded even if they've already eaten eleven eggs. Not a bad deal. Grocery stores have been collecting them. We're in charge of all the Food Leopards in Broward. Technically, we're supposed to drive the rotten eggs to Orlando and drop them off at a special incinerator. Sharma says the brass are too busy putting out fires and don't really care how they're destroyed as long as they disappear. So we don't have to drive mid-state."

"Wait, what are we doing?" I say. I'd kind of tuned Frank out. Sometimes I get motion sickness.

"We're like a sinister Easter bunny. We gather eggs and dump them where they'll never be found."

"All right. Where?"

"There's this place in the Glades where I fish sometimes. It's remote. We'll unload them into the swamp. The gators will be pleased. It's a win-win. Plus an extra win. Everyone's happy. Maybe even you."

———

The eggs are neatly stacked on pallets in the back by the loading dock waiting for us. Frank tells me to be careful. He's spread newspaper on the bottom of the van in case they break. While I get to work, he enters the store to track down the manager. He mentioned there's paperwork involved.

One thing I know how to do is lift properly. This isn't something everyone knows. I learned my lesson the hard way when I first started bussing. I'm pretty thin and am getting thinner. My muscles are puny. When I flex my biceps, you can't tell I'm flexing. It looks like I need to use the bathroom. I keep my spine straight and lift with my knees to avoid back strain. These eggs are a piece of cake. They're in light blue Styrofoam cartons. I stack them in the van like a pro. I used to be decent at Tetris. Dad always counted on me to arrange the luggage in the trunk when we'd go on family vacations. If I ever let money back into my life, I should get a job at the airport loading cargo. Or maybe I could become a bricklayer. I'd get thick arms. Eventually everyone would call me Bricks.

Right around the time I'm done, Frank returns. He does a quick inspection to make sure the stacks are stable, pats me on the back, and says, "*Egg*celent work, man."

"Oh, Christ," I say. "How do you still have a girlfriend?"

"I've got skills," Frank says, winking. "Sharma would dig that joke. It'd crack her up."

Back in the van, on the way to the next Leopard, the stench is heavy. A lot of people think rotten eggs smell like sulfur but I don't think that a lot of people have smelled sulfur. I haven't, that's for sure. If anyone asked me I'd compare the scent to vinegar or maybe formaldehyde. Like the frogs we dissected in high school.

"Hey, Frank," I say, "did you do the egg drop when you were in school?"

Frank has a weak chin, which he tries to hide beneath a patchy goatee. He scratches the back of his neck and leaves a streak of newspaper print there. "Yeah. From the bleachers," he says. "Mine busted."

"Same. Did they make you carry an egg wrapped in tissue paper and pretend it was a baby? To scare you away from sex?"

"No. We used a bag of flour. It didn't work."

"Oh, yeah. That's right. It was a flour baby. Mine was punctured by lunch."

At the second Leopard, I ask Frank to get me a bottle of water when he disappears into the air-conditioned store and leaves me in the sweltering heat. A few of the employees lounge on a dilapidated picnic bench near a canal. They smoke and glare at me. A gang of mean-looking ducks picks at discarded butts. They don't want to have anything to do with me and these bad eggs.

On our way to the next store Frank announces we have three more stores to go. It's only after we've arrived at the third Leopard and he is disappearing again that I remember I asked for a bottle of water that he and I have both forgotten. Luckily, there's a worn, gray-colored garden hose coiled poorly next to a dumpster. The hot water burns going down.

One time when I was a kid, I found an Easter egg under our china cabinet the Bunny had hidden the year before. The blue dye had faded to gray. It was lighter than the other eggs. Tiny hairs of mold, which looked like fur, covered the shell. I delicately carried it in cupped hands to my mother. Horrified by the sight of the moldy egg, and incredulous that no one had noticed it all year, she declared it rotten. "Get rid of it," she said.

But I didn't get rid of it. I stood over the garbage can in the kitchen turning it over in my hands. The egg was unusual, but it didn't seem spoiled. When I put it under my nose, I couldn't smell anything. It had lost its odor. When I placed it next to my ear and shook it, I heard a faint rattle, as though the yolk had shriveled to the size of a coin. When I licked it, the egg had a coppery flavor, like tasting pennies or blood.

Though I wanted to know what a bad egg looked like inside, I couldn't bring myself to crack it open. I put it back exactly as I'd found it. My plan was to inspect it again next Easter, but I couldn't wait. When I checked a few weeks later, it was gone.

———

On our way to the fourth Leopard, Frank's cellphone rings, which reminds me that I have mine in my pocket. I keep it on vibrate and haven't felt anything. He's got a jaunty Bob Marley ringtone. When he picks up and talks to Sharma—I can tell it's her by the way Frank softens his voice—I inspect mine. It's still dead.

"All right," Frank says before hanging up. "I'll see what I can do."

Frank's quiet for a while. I can tell he's thinking about something because he keeps stroking his goatee. A fly alights on my elbow. I don't know if it flew in from outside or if it was hiding with the salmonella-flavored eggs. Finally, he says, "That was Sharma."

"Yup," I say, swatting.

"She's waiting for me at our last stop."

"Cool." The fly positions itself on the dashboard. There's a section of newspaper at my feet, which I roll into a baton.

"It will nearly be dinner time when we get there."

"Already?" I say, distracted. When I spring, the fly darts away.

"I haven't seen her in a week."

"Oh." I concentrate on the empty spaces inside the van. In my experience, it's better to anticipate where a fly might go rather than trying to track where it's been.

"Look," Frank says. "I thought I might take her to dinner and then crash at her place for the weekend. We both have off, which is rare. She needs to unwind from the egg debacle."

"You guys sound serious." The fly lands on Frank's headrest. It's inches from his ear.

"I wonder if I could trust you to finish the job on your own. I could kick you an extra Grant. Could you be the Bad Bunny for me? For us?"

In order to crush the fly, I'd have to whack Frank across the head. If I did, he'd lose control and we'd flip and roll into the ditch. Then our big, white van-egg would crack and we'd drown in a pool of yolk.

"Sure," I say.

I fight back the urge to murder the fly.

———

Frank helps me load the eggs at the remaining stores. Suddenly he's in a hurry. By the time we get to the final Leopard, the van is completely packed. I even have to jam a carton in the glovebox. There must be five thousand eggs inside. It's probably some kind of record.

Before hustling to meet Sharma, Frank hands me the keys and a map he's scribbled in the margins of a newspaper. "I appreciate it, Bricks," he says.

"No problem."

"You know, Blue Zephyrs is busting at the seams. It's nearly impossible for me to keep up with my newspaper route. I have enough business to deliver all week. Maybe you'd be interested in picking up Tuesdays and Thursdays and sometimes Saturdays. You can borrow my van until you're able to buy your own ride."

"Maybe," I say, staring at my shoes.

"Leave the keys in the glovebox. I'll swing by early Sunday." When he pats me encouragingly on the shoulder, my shoulder disappears beneath his huge hand. "Think about my offer."

I do think about becoming a newspaper deliveryman as I drive slowly south along I-95. The squeaking from the Styrofoam cartons rubbing together sounds like helium balloons having an orgy. From the interstate, I take a highway. Off the highway is a county road. A half-mile from a gas station I find the unnamed dirt road Frank sketched on the map. I see a crooked cypress with branches in the shape of a number four, which is where I'm supposed to turn and begin the off-road portion of the journey. The dirt road is one-way and rutted with tire tracks. It's the kind of path motocross racers and monster truck enthusiasts frequent. I have to slow to a crawl to keep the eggs from tipping.

I don't know how I'd accommodate the super-early hours if I take Frank up on his offer. That's only part of the problem. I'd also be forced to interact with old people and old people frighten me like nothing else. When I used to bus tables at the diner, I became intimately familiar with the bits and pieces of half-masticated morsels old patrons couldn't quite swallow and left in a wet lump upon their plates. No amount of scrubbing can clean those dishes from memory. Also, old people are the only generation that still uses pennies. They like to leave a nest of them for a tip on the sticky tabletop.

Still, I'm not really in a position to turn down a job. Moping around doesn't pay well. I suppose I could rearrange my sleep pattern. I'd probably see sunrises. Outside of the diner, ancients might be better. Like they say about sharks and snakes, maybe the elderly

are just as scared of me as I am of them. Perhaps, once we're acquaint-
ed, we'll find we have things in common. They've been abandoned
by their families and I was abandoned by my ex. We could bitch and
moan together and then get over it by playing bingo and shuffleboard. I'd make a temporary friend. The two of us could eat poached
eggs and sip Ovaltine. I'd read him the obits and study his leathery
parchment face when I mentioned a name he recognized. I'd listen to
him shape stories around his fleeting memories. And when my friend
died I'd befriend another soon-to-be-dead old dude and explain how
swell my most-recently-deceased old friend was. Then the new friend
would die and I'd make another old new friend, and so on and so
forth until one day I was gone. Maybe I'd meet someone willing to
say something nice about me.

Beyond a tight corner the road opens up and the swampy shoreline unravels around a vast expanse of water. A weather-whipped pier
juts into the murk. People probably launch their airboats and canoes
from here. This is the place where Frank has drawn an X on the map.

I make a neat semicircle and back up to the water's edge. Then
I get out and stretch. Above, serious clouds dominate the sky. Rain
is on its way. Daylight squeezes through mangrove trees and purples
the calm water. Something sizeable splashes near a cluster of swamp
knees. It could be a bass. I don't fish but I'm willing to learn if Frank
invites me.

Walking to the shoreline, I notice that I've backed up too far. I
can't open the van doors without standing in the water. Luckily, it's
shallow enough for me to wade in. I ball my socks, stuff them in my
shoes, and cram them between the stacked eggs in the passenger seat.
Then I step in and throw the doors wide.

I pluck an egg from a carton and hold it in the fading light. It's
too bad nothing is going to hatch from it. Then again, the Everglades
is no place for a chicken. I can think of a dozen animals that would

devour it in a heartbeat. Up close, I see the shell has pores and microscopic veins. It's moist from all the humidity. I guess it's diseased but it looks fine to me.

Winding up, I hurl it as far as I can. It soars through the muggy air like a comet and makes a pleasant-sounding plop in the water when it lands. I get to work. I fling two, three, four eggs at a time. When they crack, the goo runs through my fingers and streaks down my arms. I hear a rumble of thunder. Mosquitoes drape me with lust. I smash them with my eggy hands. Soon, I'm a bloody mess and tired as hell and I've barely made a dent. I rest for a moment on the bumper.

About five yards out, all the broken yolks in the water have formed a stain kind of in the shape of a body. It's got outstretched arms, long legs, and a watermelon-sized head. Feasting minnows disturb the skin of the swamp, causing the figure to shake and dance. It's yearning to come alive. I wish it would rise up, skim to shore, and have a seat next to me. The stain and I would soak it all in: the psychopathic crickets buzzing like chainsaw murderers; the sharp, ragged screech from a raptor soaring beneath the blanket of clouds; the intimate mosquitoes happy in the hollow of my ears. There's vibrancy in the very air. An electric anticipation crackles from the sky, a pulsing thrum bubbles up from the swift fish, and a quivering bloodlust radiates from the nocturnal predators in the brush hungry for impending darkness. Everything is buzzing and humming. Even me.

Then I realize my cellphone is vibrating.

Standing, I take the phone from my pocket. Sure enough, the screen is bright. I have two voicemail messages. The first one is from my mom. She hasn't heard from me in a while and is worried. The second is from Mr. Oliver, my boss at DinerLand. I'm fired.

That's it. Nothing from the ex. Nothing from her because there will never be anything from her. I'm an idiot to think otherwise.

"Cluck it," I say, and throw my phone again. This time I cast it with conviction. It flies farther than any egg and plunks loudly near a family of water lilies. Good riddance. Let it rot in the bog.

The rain begins to splash down as if it was politely waiting for me to finish my tantrum. It feels refreshing. I get clean. My yolk-stain friend is obliterated.

I snatch entire cartons of eggs, dump them in the shallows, and jam the empties back in the van. The storm rages. I'm drenched. By the time I'm done, it's dark and drizzling. I've created an enormous egg island that rises out of the water and looks like a tombstone. May all this wasted food rest in peace.

After putting my shoes back on, I crank the engine. But the van doesn't budge. I lean down on the accelerator and the motor growls, but I can't move forward. My rear wheels are stuck. I throw it in reverse and quickly shift to forward hoping I'll be able to rock out of the pit I've created. The tires spin, and I only lurch a few inches before sinking again. Clicking the headlights on, I step outside to survey the damage.

It's difficult to see in the dark. Then a bolt of lightning illumi-nates the night and my attention is drawn to the water where many marbles of light appear on the surface. They instantly wink off in the aftermath of the flash. I'm not certain what I just saw. I'm no swamp expert. It could have been some kind of optical illusion or a flock of pixies. Maybe it's the will-o-the-wisps, whatever those are. When the sky brightens again, the marbles return. This time, two of them a few feet in front of me don't disappear. In the red glow of the taillights, I figure it all out. These are alligator eyes gather-ing in the lightning and spitting it at me. A congregation of them. Advancing.

I hurry inside the van. I remove the keys so I don't drain the engine and then climb into the back. If I had my phone, I could call for help. Really, though, who would I call? No tow truck would drive back here. And I can't call Frank. He's out having a romantic evening. The last person he wants to hear from is me living up—or down—to my nickname. There's nobody to call and nothing to call nobody with. I'm stuck in the mud surrounded by alligators chomping diseased eggs. I can hear them grunting and hissing as they thrash and gorge. Their thick tails could lash out and bust the van open. A dark, tired, helpless part of me wishes they would—embrace me in a death roll and squeeze me into a stain.

———

In the morning, I awaken to sunlight and birdsong. Despite a pinched nerve in my neck, the angry spray of mosquito welts, and a deep hunger, I feel rested. Empty egg cartons make a good pillow.

Outside, the day is underway. The alligators are gone, as are the eggs. A few shell fragments cling to weeds along the shore.

The tires are nested deep in the mud. There's no way I'll be able to shove my way out. My limited experience with cars came from an auto mechanics class in high school. For a short while, my parents encouraged me to pursue a career as an automotive technician. Then there was an incident when I tried to yank out an oil plug and kicked over the jack stand and nearly got my head crushed. After that, Mom and Dad steered me toward less dangerous occupations like accounting, business administration, and real estate.

Back then, when my parents asked what I wanted to be when I grew up, I'd say I didn't know. I discovered when you wait long enough without wanting to be anything, you eventually become a disappointment.

One thing I did learn before getting kicked out of auto mechanics is if you slide the car floor mats between the mud and rubber tires, you can create traction and get unstuck. It takes a few tries, but eventually I angle them right and, with a little coaxing, guide the van out.

When I'm on the highway, I notice the time: 7:47. Like the airplane. And yeah, thinking about airplanes reminds me that my unfaithful ex flew away with that timeshare guy, but that's all right. Now it's 7:48. Early for me, but I'm wide awake. Maybe I will take Frank up on his offer. It's nice to drive his van. The two of us have been through something meaningful. We survived the night.

At home, after I've parked, I open the glovebox to put the keys inside and discover the carton of eggs I'd jammed there. I forgot all about them. I have become my own Easter Bunny. Only five of the eggs are intact. I carefully carry them to my apartment and crack them into a pan. Then I retrieve the toaster from the windowsill and set it on the counter. When I plug it in, I don't die. I grab the bread from the freezer and jam two slices into the slots. I force the lever down. The eggs scramble themselves.

If only Mom could see me now. Her boy making breakfast. With a functioning toaster. Wearing pants. With some cash in my pocket. About to sit down and eat and think about what I'm going to do with my day. With my tomorrow and next week. I'll make plans for my future just like every other idiot in the world.

MRS. HUTCHINSON'S BONES

after Shirley Jackson's "The Lottery"

THE MORNING OF JUNE 27 was overcast and gloomy outside the town. Beyond the cobblestone streets, the sleepy fields stretched to the bank of the river. Across the water was the forest. Nobody in the village knew what was beyond the trees. Just downstream, at Jackson Falls, water crested over the horizon and dropped two hundred feet to the boulders below. Mist rose from the churning basin.

A flock of grackles skittered out of a cornfield when they sensed the vibrations from thundering footfalls. In platoons they took to the sky, darted across the swift water, and perched in the high branches of sycamore, birch, and pine. From that vantage, as soon as the haze blazed away, they could see everything.

In the village it was clear and sunny. People arrived to the square early for the selection. Though good-natured, a sense of dread clutched at the hearts and throats of the citizens until, finally, everyone learned the name of the chosen one. Then the anxious energy morphed into enthusiastic bloodlust.

This year—which would be the last—Mrs. Hutchinson drew the slip of paper with the coal-black dot. Since she'd participated in many ceremonies, she understood what came next. Knowing this didn't stop her from protesting. "It isn't fair," she said as the villagers moved in on her.

That's what they all said—*It isn't fair, it isn't right.* It was the lament of the doomed. Mrs. Hutchinson did what her predecessors always did; she clenched fists, spit, cursed, and punched wildly at her encircling neighbors. The quick children flitted along the periphery and hurled stones with practiced accuracy. From bruised knees the victim ordinarily attempted reason. *If you spare me, I'll mend your fence, Mr. Bentham. You can have my chickens, Mr. Graves. I'll paint your barn, Mr. Summers. Mr. Warner, I'll check on you at night from time to time to make sure you're not lonely.* The list was exhausted rather quickly. It was a modest village. There was no bargaining. As the saying went, "Sacrifice in June, corn grows heavy soon." Mrs. Hutchinson knew this. In fact, she taught it to the children at the schoolhouse. "If you don't follow the path of tradition," she'd lectured, "you stray into ruination. Count your blessings, kids."

Mrs. Hutchinson's blessings were gone. Most sacrifices, after beaten into delirium, hissed prayers through cracked teeth until their final, ragged breath was drawn. The mashed bodies were buried beneath a neat mound of polished quartz upon a hill upriver that, as everyone in town knew, offered the most spectacular views. From on high you could see thatched rooftops, verdant gardens, and the lucky, bustling inhabitants. Though they rarely visited the burial ground, from time to time townsfolk lifted their heads, massaged their aching lower backs, and squinted up the hill to fondly recollect the men and women who had donated their lives for the betterment of the community.

Unlike the others, Mrs. Hutchinson was not ready to concede defeat. With the deepest conviction she felt—she *knew*—the process had been tainted. Rigged, even. "It isn't right!" she howled.

Nobody was surprised that Tessie refused to accept her fate with dignity. She was stubborn as a plague of locusts. She possessed an unnatural and nuanced rage which made her a fantastic disciplinarian in the classroom but a challenge to interact with socially. If you so much as looked at her the wrong way, she was liable to singe you with a sharp word or two. Some folks claimed she clung too tightly to the notion that they lived in a moral and just world. "Tess," her husband often said, "sometimes things just are what they are."

"You're a damned fool, Bill," Mrs. Hutchinson would reply, even in mixed company. "Good's balanced with evil. Right's squared with wrong. Honor what was and tomorrow'll be better. How could you get up in the morning believing otherwise?"

Most mornings Bill had difficulty getting up, on account of the arthritis.

After she drew the doomed slip of paper, Tessie's blood boiled with indignation. She just knew, in her bones, something was wrong. Maybe it was sabotage. Someone could have tampered with that old black box. Surely a dirty worker from the coal company knew the combination to the safe, and where Mr. Summers kept it, and stole in late last night and tore a tiny corner off the marked slip so he and his friends could avoid it. Also, Bill had been rushed. "You didn't give him time enough to choose. *Every*body saw that," she said. "If he'd had more time…and why don't they use wood chips anymore? That's what they used to do. Who changed the rules? Why not return to the old tradition? Life had been better then…and Mr. Delacroix peeked. I saw him, I swear. Where's Clyde Dunbar? His leg was fine. He was limping around the lawn last night. He could have hobbled here and drawn like a man instead of forcing Janey to stand in for him. The slip was meant to be his. I demand a redo!"

Nobody listened to Mrs. Hutchinson. Collectively, they had stopped thinking of her as Mrs. Hutchinson. Her voice, her identity, her history, all of that was stripped away. She was simply the sacrifice. It was better for the children to think this way.

As long as she never drew the dreaded slip of paper, it was easy for Tessie to believe in fate. As the chosen one, it didn't make sense.

If only the mob would give her a few more minutes to think, she'd figure it all out and explain. There was a perfectly reasonable explanation for the mix-up. But time and reason had vanished. All Tessie had left was animal instinct. A guttural growl erupted from her dry lips: "It isn't right, it isn't fair!"

Later, Steve Adams, who was on the front line, swore Tessie's blue eyes flashed scarlet right before she leapt to her feet and shoved him a meter back. "She was aided by some powerful evil, that's for sure."

Mrs. Hutchinson broke through the throng, sprinted past the post office and bank, and tore into the fields. Birds scattered. The fleetest teens gave chase. Jack, fast as a fox, took aim, cocked his arm, and threw a stone he'd been sharpening for weeks. That projectile, from fifty feet, shaved a hairy chunk of scalp from the top of Tessie's head. Later, Jack boasted that her noggin looked like it'd been shucked. Held on by the thinnest of ligaments, the skin flap wetly flopped against the nape of her neck. After a few dizzy paces, the rapid blood loss disoriented the quarry. She stumbled into a tight row of corn and collapsed. Several boys trampled a circle in the crop around the victim to make room for the others. It was considered bad luck if you didn't strike the sacrifice with at least one rock, and the youth of this village had enough respect for their elders to give them a turn.

Right there, in that precise spot on the earth, was where Tessie would have been bludgeoned to death if it weren't for the grackles. The fog covering the field dissipated, and the birds took notice of the violent human affair unfolding in the crops. What did they see? It's impossible to say for sure. Men are not black birds with iridescent wings. What did they do? Well, they didn't swoop low and peck out the eyes of the attackers. They didn't, as a unit, air lift the lightheaded woman to safety. They didn't beckon a pack of snarling wolves. Instead, one grackle simply cawed, *It isn't fair*. Another bird—trees away—replied, *It isn't right*. Soon, the rest of the flock pitched in, calling and responding louder than the rumble of the river. When the message vibrated into Mrs. Hutchinson's blood-crusted ears, she muttered, "Yes. True. It isn't." Under a fierce volley of stones, she found the courage to stand.

Later, Mrs. Hutchinson's son Davy admitted he had the strongest urge to tackle his mother and hold her down. Like the other children, he had been taught not to touch the chosen ones or else you might be chosen soon yourself. Even though kids didn't draw until they came of age, they heeded the warning all the same. Since the older children were running out of rocks, Davy handed his pebbles to them and stared at the fleeing sacrifice with his big blue eyes.

Mrs. Hutchinson careened through the stalks, staggered out of the field, and waded waist-high into the river. She stood swaying in the water, chanting. Nobody but the birds understood what she was saying.

Along the bank were plenty of rocks. Caught up in the thrill of the hunt, Harry pried a slab the size of a newborn hog from the sucking mud. He tottered knee-deep into the water, hoisted the stone above his head, and heaved it at his prey.

Tessie fell face first into the river. The onlookers let out a cheer that she didn't hear. She didn't swim or kick against the current. Her filthy yellow dress billowed. Blood mixed with water, water with blood. The merciful river carried her over the falls and snuffed out her life on the jagged boulders below. She bobbed in the agitated eddy for a short while before the current tugged her under. Above, the villagers watched her body float away.

"Well," Mr. Summers said. He was nearly out of breath from the chase. "Let's get back to work."

And they did, indeed. They piled a mound of quartz upon the hill next to the other sacrifices. After a while, nobody even remembered that Mrs. Hutchinson wasn't buried there.

———

The body washed ashore five miles downstream, where the river elbowed. It was a popular place for animals to drink. At dusk, under a sliver of moon, a pair of raccoons discovered the carcass. After a short tussle, the bigger scavenger chased the littler one away. The commotion and tantalizing scent of fresh blood attracted a bobcat. The queen swatted the snarling coon aside and dragged her bounty deep into the woods, where hungry cubs waited. They feasted on the soft innards all night and left the scraps in a thatch of clover for the vultures. The carrion-eaters efficiently ripped apart the tough sinew and gristle and gorged. Their stained beaks were painted into smiles. Once they were sated, the rodents scuttled out of holes and crevices. Rat teeth and tongue picked clean all traces of flesh. Then the insects arrived.

After a few days, there was nothing left between Mrs. Hutchinson's skeleton and dust but time. The summer sun baked the earth, autumn gusts stripped the leaves, December snow blanketed the forest floor, and from the wet, vernal earth the fortified clover grew. While people busily buzzed from decision to decision, nothing changed in the woods along the edge of the river a few miles from Jackson Falls.

One summer morning, nearly ten years later, Mrs. Hutchinson's rotting skull released a malevolent force that had been stored in the marrow. Primal hatred Tessie didn't know she possessed was imprinted into her organic bone tissue. It had been dormant in life, but in death the fury was just waiting to be unleashed by decomposition.

The malice started in the jawbone. Heat crackled from her putrid mandible and set the detritus into which she had settled aflame. The wildfire torched 25,000 acres. It leapt over the river and razed the cornfields and crops that had sustained the village for so long.

Ash coated the land in a sulfuric gray blanket. Smoke choked countless animals. Citizens coughed for weeks. Mrs. Hutchinson's bones
smoldered.

Once the air cleared, the villagers gathered together and gazed
at the open space where the forest used to be. "So that's what's over
there," Mr. Summers said from the falls. "It's just like what's over
here." He scratched his liver-speckled bald head and said, "Let's get
to work."

Many of the early settlers to the new town were miners, carpen-
ters, and factory workers. Horace Dunbar bought three acres of land
and moved his wife and son to the new settlement. He planted straw-
berries, and in no time, the ripe fruit leapt from the nutrient-rich
soil. Horace should have been happy. He should have appreciated the
plentiful yield of the crop. The problem, though, was that he couldn't
figure out why one small square of earth remained infertile. The dead
patch wasn't particularly large—roughly three square yards—but it
happened to fall in the middle of an otherwise robust row. He tried
a variety of fertilizers on the soil and tilled it until his fingers bled.
Still, nothing. Then one May afternoon, when he was over-seeding
the spot, he had a brain aneurism and collapsed. Through a window
in the kitchen at their house, Mrs. Dunbar witnessed her husband
clutch his head, drop to his knees, and fall face first into the agitated
dirt.

People felt badly for Kitty's loss. Horace was still relatively young,
taken—sympathizers cried—before his time. Townsfolk shook their
fists at the cruelty of fate. Then, one breezy morning in October, the
string from a polka-dotted kite was yanked out of eight-year-old Brian Dunbar's clutching hands. From the porch, Mrs. Dunbar watched
her son chase the skittering thread over the wilting strawberry plants.

Afterward, Kitty would try to explain what she saw with her own
eyes—which people wouldn't believe, the haughty dismissal driving

her in mid-November to slit her wrists in the spot where she saw what happened happen. She'd said, "The kite stopped in midair as if waiting for my son." When Brian breathlessly arrived, a microburst whipped up out of the ground and twirled the thread around and around his pale neck until it squeezed the life from him.

In the aftermath of the tragedy, Betty Zanini, a friend and member of the church to which the Dunbars belonged, organized a small congregation to hike into the field and place three wooden crosses where the Dunbar family had perished. A half-dozen people were able to make it. More of the congregation would have attended if it wasn't for the cold snap. After driving the markers into the reluctant ground, everyone prayed. It was so frigid that the words froze the moment they escaped blue lips. In the morning, every one of the mourners woke up without eyesight. Blinded, they couldn't see the crosses they'd planted had been ripped from the ground and rearranged into bundles of stick figures tied with kite string and littered across the barren field.

These strange phenomena spooked the superstitious citizens, and rumor spread that the Dunbar place was cursed. For years, the town grew up around the property. The population expanded and people prospered. The mayor of the modest-sized city decided to use public funds to purchase the old Dunbar farm and convert it into a nice park where families could picnic and throw a football with spirited children. Since the groundskeeper couldn't get any grass to grow over a certain patch of ground, the Planning and Zoning Board simply had a park bench erected. Upon that bench couples argued, businessmen were mugged, a black widow climbed into a young woman's water bottle, and Mr. Allen choked to death on a hotdog. Soon, the park was abandoned by happy families and inhabited by degenerates. The police chief lost count of the number of alcoholics and drug addicts who expired in a gurgle of despair.

In an effort to turn the negative space into a positive one, Mayor Graves paved a large portion of the park and built a library. Other than one incident—a construction worker was crushed by a pile of lumber that had been poorly stacked—the Jackson Public Library was completed on schedule. It opened on a sunny morning in late June.

Inside, the smell of fresh paint and new books permeated the bright air. Children paged through vividly colored picture books while adults browsed the bestsellers. A modest crowd milled through the stacks and fingered the spines of hardbacks.

Toward the rear of the library, in the media room, were several computers. Each monitor rested in its own partitioned carousel to provide privacy. This section soon became the most popular area of the library. Although everyone had their own computer at home, there was something that drew them to the media room. People could browse however they chose without having their IP address traced. There was freedom in the anonymity. The space became so popular, patrons would camp in front of the monitors all day. Under a volley of complaints, Ms. Percy, the librarian, had to set a two-hour time limit so everyone could have a turn.

Over one particular computer station, the florescent light always flickered. The maintenance workers replaced the bulb and rerouted the wires, and still the light blinked and hissed. People didn't mind. In fact, many visitors preferred to sit at that particular station. Half lit, the area afforded additional privacy. Plus, the low, erratic, eruption of sound was oddly pleasant. It was familiar and peaceful like distant traffic. Users incubated in a comfortable numb.

If someone had the willpower to shift their attention from the screen and actually listen, they might detect a pattern bleating from the flashing light and buzzing static. If they allowed the vibrations to trickle into their ears, they might detect a broadcast, an electronic cry on an endless loop: *It isn't fair. It isn't right.*

Nobody heard the message. Nobody mustered the courage to stand, power down the computer, flip the light switch off, and sprint outside into the vast open world.

Mrs. Martin, a spritely octogenarian who'd outlasted four husbands, teetered to the computer each morning at 8:45. She set her ebony cane against the wall beside her and visited www.sewimpressive.com. The site was created for the modern seamstress. On it, you could learn new patterns, best stitching practices, and tips for accurate sewing. Because building a community was important to the woman who hosted the site, there was a blog where people shared stories and pictures. That's where Mrs. Martin spent her time. Hunting and pecking for the right keys on the keyboard, she would reply to a picture a seamstress had proudly posted by writing: *Mrs.Sewand-Sew, the thumbs in your mittens are lopsided. Maybe you should try a different hobby, dear.* To this insult, Mrs.SewandSew responded: *I'm trying my best, BadBird5000. And for your information, my husband loves my sewing. He's wearing the mittens right now and says he can't wait for it to get cold!* Mrs. Martin, shielded by her alias, wrote: *You must have stitched your husband's eyelids shut because he'd have to be blind to think you had any talent. He's also having an affair with your sister and feels sorry for you.* Mrs.SewandSew replied: *You are rude and inappropriate. Shame on you! You don't know anything about me. I'm reporting you to the webmaster.* Excitedly, Mrs. Martin wrote as quickly as her old fingers could clack: *Die! Die! Die! You stupid bitch!* And then the community portion of the site shut down, and Mrs. Martin would visit another site and scroll down the comments section. Eventually, the librarian would gently tap Mrs. Martin on the shoulder and inform her that her time was up. A line was forming.

The moment Mrs. Martin was gone, the next visitor slid into the still-warm seat. It could be Mr. Anderson, who hated felines. He'd search pictures of cats or kittens on social media. The happy pet owner might post a photograph of a tortoiseshell-coated tom chasing its tail with a note that read: *Keep trying, Fritzy, you can do it!* To this, Mr. Anderson would copy and paste an image of a bagful of cat carcasses along a muddy riverbank attached with the note: *I'm coming for your pussy.*

When his time expired, Joey Watson would take his place. Except for the two hours allotted to him while he sat at the public computer, Joey really wasn't a racist. Barbara Jones was *IHateU351.* She blasted romance novels she'd never read on GoodReading.com and enjoyed calling both authors and readers fat sluts. Greg Clark, who showed up in the late afternoon, took great pains to replace lyrics and graphics to popular children's tunes. He'd re-record songs and post them on YouTube. If a kid decided to click on "Row, Row, Row Your Boat," they might be exposed to: "Row, row, row your butt, gently with a spoon. Merrily, merrily, merrily, merrily, anal sex is fun!" while pornographic images interrupted the otherwise pleasant video. Parents complained like hell in the comments section.

Old Man Warner was usually the last in line. He stood fidgeting just outside the circle of humming light. When it was finally his turn, he'd scour the web for obituaries and write, where grievers expressed sympathies for the families and friends of the deceased: *I'm thankful your loved one is gone. It's your fault. You should be ashamed. The dead will hate you for all eternity.*

Beneath his feet, beyond the carpet, concrete, and dirt, Mrs. Hutchinson's bones radiated as they slowly decomposed.

Though Old Man Warner and the rest of the users would never know it, the vicious remarks they made spread seeds of malice across the planet. The victims might be angry at first, and cry, "What kind of person could ever write something so mean?" Certainly not them. After a while, once they calmed down, they would grow despondent. They'd quit visiting the sites that once gave them pleasure.

They might ride a bike, go fishing, or work on a crossword puzzle, anything to keep their minds preoccupied. Sooner or later, though, their resolve would begin to crack. They'd start to resent the faceless monsters that spoiled their enjoyment. Then, one by one, they'd get their revenge by visiting the local library and waiting in line for their turn at the public computer. They'd chisel words into stones and hurl them into cyberspace. Afterward, they wouldn't feel good, but they'd feel justified.

Around 9 p.m., the Jackson Public Library closed. The janitor rearranged chairs, emptied trash cans, swept the floors, extinguished the lights, and locked the front door. Back home, everyone did what they always did: watched television, ate a bowl of ice cream, brushed teeth, and went to bed. In dreams, their guilty ancestors maddeningly chattered. In the morning, a crowd gathered on the marble steps of the library. Citizens exchanged pleasantries and kept a close watch on the entrance. When the door was thrown wide, there was a wild rush past the towering stacks of dusty classics, around the children's craft table, and into the media room. Then the anxious energy morphed into enthusiastic bloodlust. Once the mob spotted the computer beneath the epileptic overhead light they were upon it.

ERASE THE DAYS

"WE'RE SUPPOSED TO RUN," Grant says.

It's dinner. We eat at the small round kitchen table underneath the multicolored rustic light fixture, which casts a warm rainbow glow. This is where Family Time is served. Also, it's taco night. Classical music is playing from the iWhatever on the countertop. My wife likes to keep it on when we eat. She says the music is nourishing. Like maybe, with it in the background we'll have a more inspired conversation. She didn't use that word, *inspired*, but it's what she means. I find it distracting. When a song comes on that I know, I can never quite remember the composer or the title. For me it's all Mozart and Beethoven.

To Grant I say, "That's it? Run?"

"Yeah, if there's an active ███████. Also, avoid eye contact."

"Eye contact?"

"With the perp."

"Perp?"

"Dad, yes. It's short for perpetrator."

"I know. It's just that—"

"They got a pamphlet," Heather says.

"I'd like to see that."

"It's on the kitchen counter. Beside the bills."

"For homework we're supposed to write how we feel about ██." "Feel?"

"Dad, come on. You need to get your hearing checked."

"I'm sorry. It's just…how you *feel*?"

"Maybe you could write a poem," Heather suggests.

"How do *you* feel about them, Dad?" Grant has this habit of shredding his paper napkin into tiny bits in his lap. "What poem would you write?"

I don't want to talk about it, and I certainly don't want to write a poem. Not ever and especially not during Family Time at the table with the salsa and guacamole.

Just thinking is bad enough. Of the kids. Any one of them could have been Grant. And the parents of those kids? No, no. I don't think so. Not going to discuss.

Of course, it doesn't matter that I don't want to talk about it. Everyone else does. Radio, television, newspapers, movies, computers, smartphones—pinging, whirring, infinitely ricocheting words, words, words, enough to make you numb. And images. Don't forget what it looks like. Digitally remastered. Everything crystal clear. Pictures so sharp they leave needles in your eyes.

"What do *you* think I should do if something like what happened at that school happens here?"

In the aftermath, teachers have been asked to prepare their classes. To bring ██ into the classroom as an *idea* in order to protect kids if it becomes a reality. As they did at that school, as they could in Grant's fifth-grade class.

"It won't," I say.

"Say it does."

"You know how small the odds are? Infinitesimal."

"It's more common than you think. The teacher showed us the statistics."

"Fine, it's bad. I get it. Talking about it doesn't help."

"We can't do nothing, Dad."

"Are you sure? Have we really even tried to do nothing?"

"We don't have to have this conversation tonight," Heather says.

"I don't want to have it tomorrow either. Let's just not talk about it. Ever. Not at the table and not at school. Maybe the best way to keep ████ out of the classroom is to keep them out *completely*."

"Yeah right," Grant says. "As if."

A part of me feels like launching into the speech I would have given if I had gone to the PTA meeting this week. That's usually my wife's jurisdiction; Heather's a much better P than I am. If I did go to the next one and was given the opportunity to offer my two cents, I'd say, "Let's keep ████ relegated to the textbooks." I'd use that word, *relegated*, to show I meant business. I'd talk loud and clear. Put a little boom in my voice. I'd say, "Let parents talk—or not talk— about ████ at home. Let's not overreact. Times have changed, but a child's innocence has not. Isn't it up to us to protect their vulnerability? To show them all the good in this world? There is still good in the world. *They* are what's good. Let us not forget that. Let us not taint them with the horrors and atrocities of our contemporary moment. What happened at that school…abominable. I don't presume to know what could or should have been done to prevent that kind of arbitrary senselessness. But let's not abandon reason now. Let's not frighten the kids."

That's what I would say, if I did want to talk about it. Heather reported that the PTA decided the school should—*must*—do something. So they've initiated a plan of action. Better safe than sorry, blah, blah. If there's a fire, kids are trained to stop, drop, and roll. Tornado? Line up in the hallway, curl into a ball, and protect your head. Now, in the event of an active-████ situation, they're supposed to run. That strikes me as wrong on many levels, but I refuse to bring it up. Instead, to Heather and Grant, I try to boil it down. I say, "It's like this: not talking + not thinking = no more ████ in school. Problem solved."

"That's fuzzy math."

"Fuzzy how?"

"Well, if you don't talk about or think about cockroaches, it doesn't make them disappear. Pass the sour cream."

"Pass the sour cream *what?*" Heather says.

"Please. Pass it, *please*, Mom."

"When you were a baby, we didn't talk or think about them," I say.

"He's not a baby anymore, Al."

"Did you know," Grant says, "that for every single cockroach you see, there are like a hundred you can't see hiding in the walls?"

"I didn't know that," Heather says. "How interesting. The bug man was here last week."

"Exterminator," Grant corrects.

"Touché," Heather says. She doffs a pretend cap in his direction.

"But Grant's got a point," I say, "with his cockroach metaphor."

"It's not a metaphor."

"It could be, though. Let's say you're not talking about *actual* cockroaches."

"I am. I read it in—"

"Pretend you're not. Think of cockroaches as ████. For every *actual* ████ you see, there are thousands, maybe millions of representations of them on television, in the movies..."

"Dad—"

"...in video games, cartoons..."

"Dad, I was talking about actual cockroaches."

"...in textbooks. And now for homework. You see? ████ are in our heads like cockroaches in the walls."

"That's more of a simile," Heather says.

"Like or as equals simile," Grant says.

"Yeah, but the idea is still sound. If your mind is a clean house, you have nothing to fear. Unless, of course, you do. Like at that school. That was nobody's fault except, obviously, that one rotten apple. For every bad one of us, how many good are there?"

"Are we talking about ███ or apples?" Grant shifts his eyes to his mother.

If you were to take two blue morpho butterflies, mash them into tiny balls in your fists, and cram them into my wife's orbital cavities, you'd have her eyes. The irises have a cerulean hue and swirl with flecks of ebony.

"You should use a simile in your poem," Heather says.

"Yes, but—" I say, with more to follow, when Grant shoves an enormous triangle of taco into his mouth. There is an explosion of sound as he gnashes. It's enough to drown out the classical music I don't recognize.

"It's Brahms," Heather says, even though I didn't ask. "You can hear him in the strings."

———

Weekdays I'm up early. I beat Grant's school bus by an hour. It's April in Richmond; April everywhere. Sun's still surfing the Atlantic. Light will not find me until I'm settled in my roost.

Before I can get into my car, I'm startled by a voice. I was just thinking about that missed opportunity when Grant asked me what he should do if an active ███ ever—God forbid—enters the school. If I'd wanted to talk about it, I could have said, "Lie still on the floor, and pretend you're already ███. Try to trick the monster." The response is imperfect, I know. It means I'm asking Grant to protect himself even if other kids get hurt. That's not exactly heroic, but it's the best I can come up with now, which is more than I came up with last night.

"I startle you, neighbor?" It's William Pettibone. He's difficult to see in the misty predawn.

"No," I say. "You're fine." William calls me *neighbor* because he can't remember my name, although we've been neighbors for seven years and sometimes he returns my mail when the mailman misdelivers it, but not before opening it—accidentally, he says.

"Gonna go stick your head in the clouds, huh?" he snorts. Though it's still darkish, I can see his bright white teeth.

He's talking about my job. I'm a bird compiler. I observe and record the migratory patterns of certain waterfowl in the nearby wildlife preserve. My eyes are on the river as much as they're in the sky. William has made it clear he thinks what I do is worthless. He cannot wrap his head around the idea of counting birds as a means of preservation. He's a retired plumber. In his profession, the toilet flushes or it doesn't. The faucet leaks until you make it stop leaking. Plunge, plunge, plunge until the clog is gone.

"Yeah, Bill, off to work."

"Hey, let me ask you something," he calls, placing one slippered foot upon the dewy grass. He has something in his hands. He's on the side of the driveway closest to my property. His robe is undone, and his huge eggshell-colored belly casts a pale luminescence. If I don't get away immediately, he'll cross through our lawns with his prehistoric gait, attempt to sling a meaty arm around my shoulder, and chum me up.

"In a hurry," I say, turning to my Camry and fumbling to unlock the door.

"A few buddies of mine were talking about converting some of the open space next to the clubhouse into a shuffleboard court, and

I thought maybe I'd bring it up tonight. You are going to the home-owners meeting?"

The lock, it clicks. The door. Opens. The car. I'm into. I slam him away and crank the engine. Reverse. Forward. Goodbye.

"We'd appreciate your support," Bill shouts, holding his soggy newspaper aloft. His gigantic voice awakens every dog on the block.

———

I'm in my blind in time to see first light stain the elbow of the James River a shimmering marigold sheen. The tree house, which I helped build with a carpenter employed by the Environmental Protection Agency, is made of plywood and two-by-fours. We painted every-thing sap green so it blends. When it looks like rain, I drape a cam-ouflage tarp over the canopy of branches. Today it's clear skies. I set my backpack aside, fold myself into a sitting position, and open the logbook.

Every morning I fetch the hefty record book from the on-duty ranger in the office before hiking the three miles in. At the end of the day, I return it. Mondays, Wednesdays, and Fridays it's Ranger Joe, the rest it's Ranger Susan. They're both bright young conservationists committed to living simple, unobtrusive lives. They shoo trapped flies out the window. Good, conscientious people. Salt of the earth. Most days we chat for a while about the weather, our health, flora and fauna. Upbeat, forward-thinking stuff. It's only on rare occasions that they complain. Sometimes they'll mention how they would like to change the past. They don't mean fixing the Grand Atrocities like the ███████ or ███—those are too big and the consequences of messing around with history might lead to other problems, etc. They're talking about smaller issues. Joe recently told me that an in-jured squirrel (it had been attacked by a hawk), which he'd been trying to nurse back to health since early March, ▇. If a Day Eraser existed in the form of a time machine or portal or leprechaun or wormhole, he'd go back and wave his arms around like a lunatic to frighten off the raptor. And Susan, who has only now realized she married Tom too soon, would subtract some of those earlier moments—either when she believed she was falling in love or else when she realized she wasn't—so the mess of the divorce didn't fill her occasionally unguarded heart with gloom.

It always makes me a little happy when the rangers feel compelled to share their problems with me. Not that I'd wish bad days upon them in order to make myself feel needed. It's just that I'm a good listener who is rarely asked to listen.

This morning Joe was chipper. He gave me a "hump day" high five. And then on my walk over here, after veering off the designated trail, I followed the river and, step by step, began to join the natural world. To be part of the murmuring water flowing beside me. Maybe *murmur* isn't the right word. It's difficult to describe the sound. I'd never think *gurgle*. Never say *tinkle*. It's a bit like being shushed, permanently. *Shh, shh, shh, shh*; quiet down. It's a lullaby I wish I could mimic in my head as I lie awake at night. I've had trouble sleeping lately. River music might help. Susan mentioned she has a Babbling Brook (with crickets) app on her phone that she plays at night. Maybe I should get one of those. The problem is that Heather's a light sleeper and it might bother her. On the other hand, she's never asked my opinion about playing classical music at dinner. I'm not keeping score or anything. Sacrifice is important in a strong marriage. But I wasn't thinking about sacrifice while I was walking here this morning. I was thinking about the water levels, which are still high from the snowmelt. I was enjoying the bold, heavy scent of decaying leaves along the bank. I noticed that from the pulpy detritus only the wet stem fragments remain.

My roost is twenty-five feet off the ground and built into a middle-aged sycamore. I nailed several two-by-two chunks of wood into the tree to serve as rungs. The carpenter built a low railing. We both stapled a patch of Astroturf to the plywood flooring to make it bearable for kneeling. Sometimes when it's slow, I'll use my backpack as a pillow and take a nap.

Inside my backpack I keep sunscreen, mosquito repellent, a flashlight, a wooden duck call, lunch, binoculars, a notebook, and a photograph of my family on vacation in San Francisco last year. We're standing on a hill beside a trolley, and I've got my arm around Heather, who has her arm around Grant. It's not the best picture of me. For some reason I'm squinting and they're not. Still, it's a fond memory.

Before becoming a waterfowl compiler, I was a trail monitor. I scoped out the miles of boardwalk and well-trodden paths and made sure visitors stayed on them. That position was fine, really, but I didn't like being the guy teenagers scoffed at when they were huddled in an off-limits section of the park smoking weed or giving each other hand jobs or whatever and I had to remind them—in a stern voice—to return to the designated path. I realize how important it is to monitor the park, particularly after what happened to Madeline. It's just that I hated being Mr. No Fun. I could see a future version of my son—or a previous version of myself—red-eyed, glowering at me from the brush.

When this position became available, I *carpe diem*ed it. Where I live is smack dab in the middle of the Atlantic Flyway, which runs from Maine to Miami. Chesapeake Bay is the largest estuary in the country. In conjunction with the watershed agreement, my colleagues—over a dozen compilers in observational blinds spanning the shoreline—and I monitor the migration patterns of geese, ducks, and swans. The information we gather is shared with the Migratory Bird Data Center, which covers the flyways across the country. While it's impossible to account for every goose, duck, and swan, it's our job to try.

Each bird is categorized according to its distinguishing characteristics. You're supposed to note the bird and its *sui generis* features in the logbook. For instance, TS19 is a cob tundra swan with a streak of black in its yellow beak. HM85 is a feisty hooded merganser with heart-shaped white plumage on her head. G121, a gander who grooms himself fastidiously, has one milky-colored eye. While I've never met the compilers in other regions, I know a little bit about them by the way they describe birds. Personally, to my ears, RD4671 quacks in more of an alto-soprano pitch than a mezzo-soprano one. Sounds deeper to me, like *Ack, ack, ack, ack* rather than *Eck, eck, eck, eck*. I know it's the same ruddy duck we're talking about because of the gray patch on its posterior—the other guy just hears it differently. That happens; no biggie. What's important is that we're on the same page in terms of recording. That the bird I see is the same bird he sees as it picks its way up and down the coast.

Every afternoon I upload the information into the computer database before driving home. It's a good gig, a job of great privilege that I don't take for granted. Despite what William might think, this is important work. Migrations matter. Most people who don't know or care to know about the wide variety of ducks in their own backyard can at least comprehend data. Statistics. Numbers. As ecosystems are destroyed, so are birds. When we can show how waterfowl populations are affected, the EPA can make a case for protecting habitats. It's a simple equation: steady numbers of ducks + swans + geese = greater chances of land preservation.

Out here, though, I try not to think about people or numbers. That's a major job benefit. Most of my days are golden. There really aren't many I'd erase if I could. Well, maybe one or two. One, for sure. The day I discovered SG1538.

In our park, ▮▮ are strictly prohibited. This is government-protected sanctuary. Supposed to be, anyway. Like school, I guess. That October day—the one I'd take back—I logged in, made my way to the blind, settled into a comfortable crouch, hoisted the binoculars, and did my usual morning sweep of the shoreline. Like it always does, sunlight arrived. That morning it illuminated what I thought was a plastic Walmart bag littering the waterline. When I peered closer through the lenses, everything became clear. Before climbing to the earth and doing my job, I set the binoculars aside, closed my eyes, and tried to get my heart to quit pounding.

The binoculars belonged to my grandfather. He was a pilot in World War II and used them to survey the ground before releasing "the thunder." Thankfully, he didn't often talk about the war or carpet-bombing Hamburg, but once I'd seen him raise his fist in the air and whistle through his dentures—making the sound a bomb might make as it spiraled to the ground—while slowly lowering his hand. Then he pounded his fist into his lap and exclaimed, "Kaboom!"

I'm grateful for his service, of course. ▮▮ Gramps - me = no Grant. When he presented me with the glasses, his old hands jittering like reeds in a hurricane, he said, "I hope you see a better world than I've seen through these." Like maybe some of the sights he witnessed were so bad they melted into the glass.

When I spotted SG1538 through Gramps' binoculars, I first felt really frightened, even though I hoped the splash of red on the swan's chest was a trick of the light off the water. After I realized what had happened, fear morphed to outrage. Some jackass had sneaked in after hours with a hunting ▮▮ and ▮▮ her just for the thrill of it. SG1538 left a gaggle of goslings behind. That day I clambered down, hoisted the carcass out of the water with a brittle stick, and reported it, like I'm supposed to do. In the official log, I wrote: *SG1538*: ▮▮ *by a hunter*.

I'm sure this news ruined the days of my colleagues up and down the coast. US Fish and Wildlife Service investigated the incident, but nobody was apprehended. SG1538 became another statistic.

That night during Family Time, Heather could tell there was something on my mind—I wear my heart on my sleeve, I've been told—and though I wanted to say something, I didn't want to talk about it. If I did, I'd bring everybody down. Better just me glum than all of us. So I excused myself. I hurried into the basement, where I sometimes whittle bird decoys, and I cried. Cried for SG1538, which was ridiculous. The bird needed a better identifier. I needed something more of her to hold onto. So I named her Madeline. Majestic Madeline with the curvy white wings.

Since that day, I've named every bird. I record the ID number in the proper column in the logbook—for example, CG4901—and then write *Jack* in my personal notebook. Jack's this jaunty common goldeneye that likes to spin in tiny circles after a meal. There's also Noah—B66—a taciturn bufflehead who grows skittish at his own warbling shadow rippling behind him. Charlotte, the green-winged teal, hides in the marsh. Daniel, a northern pintail I've seen grow up right before my eyes, bobs his head like he's dancing to some private concert. Olivia, Josephine, Ana, and Jessie are Canada geese who always stick together, even in thunderstorms. Their semierect wings form an umbrella against the cascading downpours. Dylan, a mallard, glides over the surface of the river and waits and waits and waits and waits before touching down—ever so gently—upon the diamond-bedazzled surface.

I don't see any birds now, which isn't surprising. They're in the marshes feeding on the spawning minnows, crabs, and frogs. Around noon I eat my lunch: a granola bar, some chips, and apple slices. Afterward I lean back and listen to the river.

———

I awaken to the sound of a woodpecker in the distance. Two hours have zoomed by. Finding the binoculars, I survey my small slice of the world.

One thing I try to overlook is a feathery crack in the left lens. I'm not sure how it got there. Gramps didn't pass it down to me with the scratch. Grant has used the binoculars in the past. From his bedroom window he can see a few of the brighter stars that outshine the streetlights. Maybe he dropped them. Probably I broke them. I kicked them while dozing or something. Who knows. I wish the crack didn't bother me so much. Wish I had more willpower, could muster the strength to focus on the swaying branches with the viridescent leaves expanding. When you stare an hour at a young bud, you won't notice anything. Stare a day, nada. But if you squint at one specific maple leaf for a week, you can see the way it begins—ever so slightly—to occupy space. To transform air molecules into a veiny, fibrous, respiring network. To be an individual before becoming just the green of the tree.

This time of year, the light changes slowly. The day doesn't sneak up on you the way it can in October. Sunlight in autumn bending through the old growth, warming the water, coaxes up eager snapping turtles. They torpedo to the surface, clamp the webbed feet of the runts, and dive into the abyss. The briefly turbulent water is tamed by the current. It happened to Lily last Halloween. The curious canvasback strayed from her flock. Gone—*snap*—just like that. In the logbook, I scribbled: *CB194: Deceased due to snapping turtle attack.*

The water along the shoreline in the fall is tannin rich from the bark slough. The hue on certain afternoons is what someone might call ███ red. I don't like to imagine it that way. I prefer the word *crimson*. I don't like to associate color with ███ because when I do, I start to think of what happened at that school. I remember all the ███ on the computer screen after I foolishly exposed myself to those viral videos. I know you can't really trust color on a screen; it's always a shade inaccurate. Like the yellow of that boy's smiley-face-emblazoned backpack. It appeared daffodil to me, but to someone else it might have looked lemon-colored. Our feeble rods and cones don't hold a candle to a swan's eyes, which can spot a grasshopper on a cattail from fifty feet. The backpack could have been chartreuse. Crayola would know. The boy—I won't say his name—wore clean white sneakers. How many words do we have for white? They were off-brand shoes from Target. He was captured in the school's security camera. Images had been filtered twice: there's the real color, then the recorded color, then the color on the screen. It's hard for me to add it all up. Actual + reproduced + re-reproduced = what, in terms of reality? It's not *not* real.

The first time I saw the event was on television. The breaking news. Like every other parent, I put down my cup of coffee and watched. I was hypnotized by the horror, lulled into imagining Grant at his own school doing whatever he was doing. In the video you could see how the boy's blue jeans kept slipping down. I remember thinking he should tighten his belt another notch. Cinch it. I wondered where the boy's father had been that morning. Hadn't he seen his son's ill-fitting pants?

Then the boy unzipped the yellow backpack and methodically did what he did. Took his time. What's the rush? Was he going to get a detention? How many days did he hurry away from bullies? How many swift demons caromed around in his skull? It's impossible to say, though experts claim he fit a certain *psychological profile*. Followed a particular *pattern of behavior*. All the talk, talk, talk in the aftermath, as if talking could have prevented the ███. ███ speak louder than words. I watched the televised recording that shows him calmly stroll to the front desk, after he'd done what he'd done, and stare into the camera without a hint of expression on his face. His mouth a thin line. ████ eyes far, far away. Then he slipped the smiley-faced backpack over his head, lifted the ████████, and pulled the ██████. A premeditated kiss-off to the world.

I was surprised the local station ran that recording. It wasn't cable or anything. I guess it's because you can't see any ██████. That's left to your imagination.

Of course, there's plenty to see online. There were many other cameras in the school. For a little while, before they took it down, you could find one particular video on YouTube. I made the mistake of watching it. I saw ███████████████████████████████
██
██
██
██
██
██
██
██
██
██
██
██
██
██
██████████████████████████████ The recording rolls on and on for eight agonizing minutes before it fades to black.

If I were a parent of one of the victims and I could rewind to that morning, I'd offer better last words than "Have a nice day at school"…not that I know what I'd say. And could it have been Grant? Yes, of course. And could still be. That's the point I tried to stress to him last night, although I couldn't really because I don't want to talk about it because what does talking do? Fatherly concern can't stop ████. I wish I was a different dad capable of deluding myself. Wish I was a brick-chinned pop who says in the aftermath, "Welp, it is what it is." Then I'd clap Grant on the back and watch an Orioles game on a breezy Saturday afternoon. Afterward we'd play catch in the backyard. On Sunday go to church, hit a movie, attend a concert, swing by the mall—and maybe there is still time for me to be a different dad. The first step is digging out my old mitt from the box in the basement when I'm down there whittling duck decoys.

For now, I'm here alone in my perch. It's April. Birds are still in eggs. Beaks are tap, tap, tapping, creating microscopic fissures. The chicks are straining to push heads through the space they've created and join this quivering world. They're not listening for the slither of moccasins along the sandy shore.

The light on the water is nickel colored. If Grant were here with me, I'd hand him the binoculars that I'll someday pass down to him and say, "Look at all this. Soak it in: The pungent mossy scent. The furtive chipmunk by that log. The ellipse of the dragonfly above that pool of standing water. The distant Morse code from a red-headed woodpecker. You understand? What's he saying? What do you hear? *Ap-ril, Ap-ril, Ap-ril.*"

He's not here. Every time I've extended an invitation, it has been declined.

I'll have to take what I get. Conversations during Family Time. I'm sure as Grant grows, our discussion topics will morph. We used to talk about recess and PE. Tomorrow it will be geometry, geography, history, algebra, and music. Then sex, drugs, politics, and the afterlife. And ████. I know I can't swerve around the subject forever. As Grant ages ██████ will age with him—assuming he isn't a victim, which, of course, he won't be. The odds are infinitesimal. Talking about it, though, seems inevitable. ████ will poison Family

Time. Sooner or later the subject will come up. I can imagine it now:

"Did you hear about what happened at that theme park in Orlando?" Grant will ask.

"Nope," I'll say, "I didn't. I don't. Heather, is that Mozart we're listening to?"

"Did you hear about what happened at the bowling alley in Wisconsin?"

"You mind passing the salt? This potpie is a little bland."

"My friend showed me some of that guy's manifesto—you know the one I'm talking about, the kid from San Diego who went to the community pool?"

"Is your chair wobbly? Mine feels uneven."

"Did you know that nearly twenty thousand students were exposed to ▆ violence last year?"

"What year are we talking about here? Where did you learn that?"

"Last year. They're predicting it'll be even higher this year. We discussed it in homeroom. Mr. McGinny brought it up after, you know, what happened at that school—"

"Right. Yeah. Hey, can you excuse me for a minute?"

"Where are you going, Dad? Into the basement again?"

I know there's bad news clouding my crystal ball. It could happen when my iWhatever vibrates six years from now with a message from Heather that will read: *EMERGENCY. Something happened at the school. Call me now.* I'll call. I'll learn that Grant's high school is under lockdown. A ▆ was discovered in the boys' locker room, and learning this, I'll skitter down the ladder, frighten a few crows, and speed home where (whoosh—thank God) I'll discover Grant and Heather in the foyer. He'll keep repeating *I'm fine* while my wife and I cling to him.

How many future days will I need to erase to protect him? How can I preserve Family Time now? I know it will eventually end. Grant will need to be nudged from the nest. He'll wing off to college and crest the horizon.

I'll stay here, in my blind, compiling and recording. Wildfowl will migrate. I will fill notebooks with names: handsome Ross, quixotic Jamie, furtive Lauren, witty Brian, brave Austin, resplendent Jocelyne, golden-throated Kevin, mischievous Matt, Cassie, Steve, Corey, Kelly, John, Isaiah, Rachel, Kyle, Dan, Zoe, Andrew, Shaylee, Gia…on and on and on and on. I will try very hard to understand what that poet meant when he said nothing gold can stay. Everything is only temporarily lovely. I will continue to believe that it matters that we rise in the morning and hunt for elusive beauty. That hope exists in the ghostly contrails of the passing birds.

How quickly it becomes twilight. Just like that, my workday is over. I fight to blink away the encroaching dark. With effort I stand and stretch. Shake out cobwebs. In the logbook I note that there was nothing to report.

———

Tonight's dinner is fish. Everyone's in a giddy mood. Heather tricks Grant into admitting he has a girlfriend (though he won't reveal her name). I say, "Attaboy," and attempt to tousle his hair. I do the dishes. The television shows inflate the family room with a swirl of color and sound. Then, nighty-night and the goodnight tuck-in. "Don't let bedbugs bite."

Later, in our bed, I toss and turn. Nothing new about that. I can't see the digital clock on my nightstand. It's blocked by a box of tissues. Our overhead fan is super quiet. Though I'm sure she's not awake, I say, "Heather?"

She doesn't reply.

"Hey, I was thinking about getting one of those nature-sounds apps on my phone. Something I can play at night. You wouldn't mind, would you?"

No answer, of course. I'm sure she wouldn't. Mind, I mean. Maybe she would even learn to like the buzz of the crickets.

"I'm going to get a glass of water," I say.

Out in the hallway, the nightlight glows school-bus yellow. The door to Grant's room is ajar. I hear him snoring softly. His breathing is deep and slow. I can hear the faintest whistle. Delicate instrument. He is as steady as a metronome.

I make my way downstairs and then into the basement. The lightbulb over my workbench hums softly. Sitting on a block of wood is a spoonbill that I've been whittling. The beak needs more sanding before it's ready to paint. When I reach for the sandpaper, I accidentally knock the duck off its perch and it loudly clatters to the floor. I stand still, holding my breath, listening to hear if I've woken anyone. I haven't. Except for the murmuring bulb, it's quiet.

When I go to fetch the duck, which has skittered beneath the workbench, I see a cardboard box marked *Al's Things* in my wife's handwriting. Inside are a few model airplanes, a tackle box, and a pair of walkie-talkies. When Grant was little and tucked into bed, sometimes I'd use the two-way radio to read him a story from my bedroom.

At the bottom of the box is my baseball glove. I've had it since I played in high school. It fits fine and feels familiar. Some of the laces are frayed and the pocket is so worn it stings to catch a fast ball. The leather smells like summer.

Grant's mitt is in the garage. I find it with a few balls in a bin on a shelf. His glove is still new and it smells like the athletic store where I bought it. That's something I'd like to change.

Before heading upstairs, I place both gloves on the kitchen table. Tomorrow we'll create a day that's worth repeating.

WHERE THE SURVIVORS ARE BURIED

I.

We are water creatures living a liquid existence. Every second, sixteen million tons of water falls while sixteen million tons of water evaporates. Humans, like sponges, absorb it all. Our bodies are sixty percent water. The brain and heart are composed of nearly seventy-five percent water. As we slosh from place to place everything we think and feel is soggy.

Southern Georgia, where water meets earth, is mud. In places, it's deep enough to bury a standing man. The Brunswick Swamp sprawls away from the ocean, like a smear, as far as the high southern sun permits. Road contractors, in 1945, decided to build around the wetland instead of fighting it. Interstate 95 bends, in a forty-mile half-circle, around the swamp before it straightens out at the Florida/Georgia border. For decades, motorists were diverted around the marsh. Then OceanNation—a water-based theme park—opened. It's the first thing people see when they enter Florida. After catching wind of the project, an intrepid real estate entrepreneur purchased a strip of the Brunswick Swamp and, with great effort, tamed it into a toll road. The Brunswick Expressway only goes one way—south—and it's straight as an arrow. For a buck, drivers save a half hour.

On June 4, the evening sky over the expressway holds smoke from the factories and paper mills downwind. The air smells like a diaper. Earlier, it rained and it will soon rain again. The woman cruising down the expressway in her blue Jetta rolls the window up after throwing the remains of her apple out.

When the truck driver stops to pay the toll, chains slip. The locks have not been properly fastened by the foreman at the paper mill. The driver, a woman in her early forties, is listening to a talk radio program and arguing loudly with the host. The man reminds her of her father, at whom the truck driver never yells.

The Brunswick Expressway only has one tollbooth. The toll worker does not hear the chains slither from the log pile stacked in the bed of the truck. He's often distracted. Sometimes his head is filled with cobwebs, sometimes it's covered in cotton candy. He dismisses the quick ache of sorrow that he feels when the truck rumbles forward as just another spike of depression, as familiar as a mosquito bite. He witnesses the chains scuttling behind, tiny sparks snapping off the concrete like children's fireworks.

To pass time, the tollbooth worker categorizes cars. June 4 is an animal day. He has seen a Rabbit, a Mustang, a Jaguar, a Bronco, and a Colt. A man driving his family from New Hampshire to Ocean-Nation in a maroon-colored Chevy Impala hands the worker a fifty and the young man returns two twenties, a five, and four singles. Later, once it's all over, the tollbooth worker will swear there was a boy buckled in the backseat, not a girl. He'll remember saying "Hi" to the kid.

The pyramid-piled slash pines resting in the bed of the Hefty Haulers lumber truck, on their way to a sister mill in Central Florida, are unbound. The truck driver coaxes the rig through gears and gathers momentum. The fifteen-foot log at the top slides backward and then forward. Red dots have been painted at the ends of the poles. A woman in a yellow Dodge Neon speeds by the truck. Then her car screeches to a halt. The truck driver is caught off guard by the stationary vehicle. She crunches the brakes and swerves to the right to avoid flattening the yellow Neon.

What might have happened if she jerked the rig to the left? That's another story. In this world, the log popped off the truck and tumbled through space. That particular log is twenty-three years old and it will become paper. First, it strikes the ground and then catapults into the sky. It soars over the baffled young man in the tan-colored pickup truck, who ducks. When it comes down, the pole is spinning like a second hand. It crashes into the maroon-colored Impala. The clock on the dash reads 7:49. The family man had just returned his wallet to his back pocket. There is no time for the man's brain to explain what's coming. There's the impact, the airbags, the clipped screams, and the flip and roll.

At the precise time that the Brunswick Expressway registers its first fatalities, a meteorologist at the hurricane center in Miami bears witness to the first nameable tropical system of the year. Arabelle. Her name, which means "yielding to prayer," was chosen a long time ago. The storm is born howling in the Bermuda Triangle. It eagerly ages.

II.

Two years ago, when Bister Hale was still living in Binghamton, New York, he and his mother went camping in the Catskills for his eighteenth birthday.

From inside the two-person tent, in the predawn gloom, Bister was awoken by a noise. It was an animal; he could hear the shuffling. For a moment, he wondered if it was a bear. The only thing between them and a possible man-killer was a membrane-thin canvas. Surely, if the bear wanted, it could rend and tear the tent and its inhabitants to shreds. Then Bister's birthday would be his deathday, and he didn't like the sound of that at all.

Outside was a deer, a medium-sized doe snuffling a patch of moss a few feet from the tent door. The dun-colored hide held tiny dewdrops, and in the first light it appeared as if the animal was shimmering.

"Look," Bister said, shaking his mother awake. "There's a deer, Mom."

That was the last good moment. From that deer sprang six ticks. One parasite dropped into the mother's shoe, which was just outside the tent flap. When she slid on her sneakers, the bloodsucker climbed up her sock. Mom and son had a nice breakfast, they hiked, they fished, watched the sunset, ate s'mores, and Bister told a scary story around an impressive campfire. By the end of the day, the tick had burrowed deep into the tender flesh on Mom's ankle and was a part of her. The Lyme disease that the parasite carried entered her bloodstream. Her body handled the disease poorly. After months of treatment, she slipped into a coma.

Bister and his father sat in uncomfortable chairs beside Mom in the cramped hospital bed. Doctors explained that many patients awaken from comas, and that when they do, several claim to remember being spoken to. "They hear voices," the doctor said, "particularly familiar ones."

Bister's father was a man of few words. Even when his wife was conscious, he didn't say much.

Bister talked. From the moment they'd arrive until the moment they were politely asked to leave, Bister said stuff. He talked about the weather. He talked about the vegetable garden she kept in the backyard. He caught her up on *General Hospital*. She loved painting so he checked out a book from the library on the great masterpieces and tried to describe what each piece looked like. This proved to be challenging. Picasso's work was impossible to translate into words.

Once, Bister tried to trick his stoic father into saying something, anything. To his mother, he said, "I'm sorry we went camping." When he spoke, he kept his father's face in the corner of his eye. "If I could have my birthday wish back, I'd use it on the bear. I wish that tick-infested doe was a carnivore and that it ate me and spared you. Wouldn't that be great? Right, Dad? Wouldn't a bear have been better?"

The father coughed into his fist and muttered something Bister couldn't hear.

A half year later, Bister ran out of things to say. By then, the house had fallen into disarray. His mute father lurched from work to home to the hospital, a man dedicated to living in a shroud.

On his nineteenth birthday, Bister climbed into his mother's Subaru—which had remained in the driveway since she'd slipped into her coma—and left. Just drove south. On the kitchen counter, he'd written a note to his father: *Call me when she wakes up.*

Now Bister makes change. He's got his cellphone on vibrate and keeps it in his back pocket, always. He's been working in the toll-booth for nearly a year; his twentieth birthday is around the corner.

A woman with a lisp hands Bister a twenty and, thumbing through the register, he returns nineteen dollars with a nod. He looks at the woman's chin instead of her eyes. This is a technique that his father taught him. It's a way to seem as if you're engaging strangers when you're really not.

A line of cars has formed. Hours on the road grind. Sunlight pings off bright hoods. Today has been celestial. He's seen an Aero-star, a Mercury, a Taurus, a Nova, and a Galaxy. Bister changes a five for a man in a Saturn who has a noticeable paper cut on his index finger. In line behind him is the blue Jetta Bister looks forward to seeing. He pushes the button to raise the tollgate, the Saturn drives forward, and Bister runs his hands through his shaggy hair.

Mindy pulls up next to the booth and flashes a half smile. She's wearing what she usually wears, a black leotard. In the backseat are a human-sized turtle shell and a pair of elbow-length green gloves. Mindy plays Tammy the Turtle at OceanNation. Her job is to hand out bubblegum and to sing with Ollie the Octopus sometimes. Those moments when she is allowed to sing with Ollie are the best. At home, in the shower, she practices the rousing bit at the end of the song: "And we all live together in the sea!" She holds the *sea* as long as humanly possible.

Mindy is two bites into a banana when she pulls next to the booth. She sets the banana in the cup holder and rolls her window down. The air-conditioned air escapes.

Bister smells coconut air freshener. It's something he can almost taste. With effort, he says, "Hi."

Mindy withdraws a flyer and two dollars from her purse. The extra dollar is for the stranger who will come behind her. At the moment there is nobody. "Hi," she replies, offering the money.

"There might be a meteor shower tonight," Bister says. "If the clouds keep away."

Mindy isn't interested. She says, "Did you hear about the accident?"

Bister did, of course. It shut the road down and backed traffic up nearly to the booth. "I did."

"Did you know," Mindy says, lowering her voice, "people lost their lives?"

Bister puts the money in the cash register. "That's what I overheard."

Mindy saw footage of the wreckage on the late news and read about it in the *Brunswick Observer*. "I'm organizing a roadside memorial," she says, "for the victims. You've got to do something. That could have been me. Could have been you, right?"

Bister agrees wholeheartedly.

"I left a message with the journalist who wrote that article. You know the one?"

"Well," Bister says.

"I'm sure you'll find time to read it soon. Anyway, I'm hoping he'll announce the memorial in the paper." Mindy thrusts the flyer into the booth. "Here," she says.

In large, bold font is the following:

Memorial service for the victims of the tragic car accident to be held tomorrow, June 8, at 3 p.m., on the scene (beneath the OceanNation billboard), along the side of the road. Anyone who has ever lost anything should attend. Bottled water will be provided.

"I'll be there," Bister says.

"Good. Would you mind putting it up in your window?"

"Of course."

"And maybe encourage people to come?"

"I don't really talk to drivers. They're usually in a hurry."

"Speak quickly. Be firm."

"Right."

"Everyone has lost someone. Sometimes they need to be reminded."

"Trust me, I know."

"And if they can't come, maybe they can pitch in a little extra for the survivor."

Bister didn't know there was a survivor. He knows he doesn't know a lot of things. Of her unwavering kindness, he is certain. Of his desire to get to know her better, there is no doubt. In her presence, he temporarily feels better. "You know, people appreciate what you do."

"What?" Mindy says.

"The extra dollar. For the stranger behind you."

"Well, good. I'm saving up my karma for a rainy day." Mindy remembers her banana and her tasked A/C. She rolls up the window, offers the same half smile she offered before, and waits for Bister to raise the gate.

In Mindy's wake is a man wearing a striped tie in a Prius.

"Go ahead," Bister says, waving the man through. "It's been taken care of."

"How's that?"

"The woman in front of you. She paid your fare."

"Really?"

Bister still has the flyer in his hands. He holds it up and says, "Have a look at this."

"No thanks. I'm not interested in buying anything."

"I'm not selling anything," Bister says, but the man is going and then gone.

Bister wedges the flyer between the rubber strip at the bottom of the window and the Plexiglas. He hopes it will do the talking for him.

When it gets dark enough, the single bulb in the booth, on a sensor, pops on. The night is busier than usual.

A pair of chefs, who replace their paper hats with fedoras when they're off duty, stop at the booth in an umber-colored RAV 4. Taking a deep breath, Bister decides to speak.

"Gentlemen," he says, "I'd like to draw your attention to this flyer."

The driver, a pastry chef, reads about the memorial. "What happened?"

"Well," Bister says, focusing on the hair on the man's chin, "I don't know exactly. There was an accident. There is a survivor."

The passenger, famous for his flambé, leans across the driver's lap and says, "Your pitch will be more convincing if you have more details."

"It's not a pitch. It's a memorial."

"Oh, honey," the driver says. "Put a little heart in your voice."

"What do you mean?"

"He means," the passenger explains, "convince us that it matters."

"People died."

"Yeah. You already said that. Anonymous death doesn't get the pulse racing. What about the survivor?"

"The survivor?"

The driver has flour on his eyebrows.

"A boy, maybe," Bister says. "I remember a boy."

"That's it? You remember a boy? How old is he? Does he have blue eyes? Where is he from? What music does he like? Does he eat pancakes? Crêpes?"

"I don't know."

"All right," the passenger says, "it's time for us to shove off. Give him ten dollars, Rudy. For the fund."

Bister pockets the money and raises the gate. He watches the taillights disappear into darkness.

When the next car comes through, Bister is better prepared. He says, as the elderly woman in a Sonata offers a handful of dimes, "I want to draw your attention to this flyer. There will be a memorial tomorrow to remember the victims of a terrible car crash. The people lost control of their car. There was one survivor, though, who would benefit from a donation, should you be unable to attend."

The woman has many wrinkles in the space between her bottom lip and her chin. "Excuse me?" she says. "I'm on my way to see my brother."

"So you won't have time to make it tomorrow."

"Make what?"

"The memorial. For the premier victims of the Brunswick Expressway. We were doing so well for so long. We're accepting donations."

"The sign says one dollar." She thrusts her fist forward and dumps the change into Bister's cupped hands. The coins are moist and warm.

Slowly, Bister becomes adept at talking to passersby. Until now, he hasn't had much reason. The average transaction time at the booth is eight seconds and within that short timeframe nobody can ever say anything of value. Now, though, he has a goal: collect money for the survivor and present it to Mindy. And maybe ask her out for coffee.

An old man in a Lexus stops at the booth. Bister recognizes him. He comes through every weekday evening on his way to church in Heron Hills, a suburb that bloomed at the mouth of the expressway. The man is a confessor: he uses the brief interval of time at the tollbooth to get stuff off his chest. Sometimes he calls Bister *bub*. "It's a damned shame," he says, "about that family."

"It is."

"I wish I could be at the memorial tomorrow, but I've got work."

"We are accepting donations."

"Really? Are you putting up a cross?"

"I don't know."

"Two crosses, really."

"We were thinking of starting a fund for the survivor."

"Money is fine. Important, too. But the spirit is mightier. It's infinite. You know what I mean?"

Bister knows better than to answer the man's question. He has no interest in talking about spirits.

"We've got some crosses at the church. I'll grab a couple and bring them by later."

"Not necessary."

"Oh, it's necessary, bub!"

Bister's not sure if Mindy would like the crosses or not. To the old man he says, "You know where to find me."

By the time Nora drives up in her yellow Dodge Neon, Bister has received promises from five people who will try to attend the memorial and he's collected fifty dollars for the survivor.

By piecing together snippets of information from passengers, Bister knows enough to offer a better pitch. To Nora, he says, "I wanted to take a moment and ask if you would be willing to join a group of kind individuals who are holding a memorial for the victims of a tragic car accident that took place…"

Nora does not want to talk about it, doesn't want to think about it.

"No," she says, paying and speeding forward. She narrowly misses the ascending gate. Nora tries to comfort her cat caged and buckled into the passenger seat. "It's going to be fine," she says. "You sure are a brave ox." Then Nora remembers that talking to Babe is no good anymore and the implications begin to overwhelm her as she chokes back her tears and tries to keep the car off the shoulder of the road.

The past few days have been a nightmare. First she nearly hit a raccoon. Second, the accident. And this afternoon, when she arrived home from tutoring a middle schooler on the world's oceans, her cat was mewing pathetically by the back door. Around his neck was a collar of detonated fireworks. Apparently someone—she's pretty sure it was one of the snotty teenagers who live up the street—tied several Black Cat firecrackers together into a necklace, which they lit and slid over Babe's head. There's a nasty ring in his bluish fur. From her home in Heron Hills, she raced to a veterinarian in Brunswick who had a topnotch reputation. The vet solemnly informed her that Babe had lost his hearing.

Nora talks to her cat all the time and she knows that he listens. Sometimes he responds with sounds of his own. A certain growl means he's hungry and he yelps when he's frisky. Now talking makes no sense. Babe will never hear the birds sing or the bugs chirp or other cat's howling at the moon. And he won't hear cars and dogs and children on the prowl.

Nora feels guilty. Because of her allergies, Babe is not an indoor cat. Too much dander turns her eyes red and makes her sneeze twenty or more times in a row. She's created a few designated cat areas—in the laundry room and by the back door—which she cleans fastidiously after Babe has taken his catnap or lunched indoors.

The half hour home passes quickly. Nora opens a can of soft cat food and lets Babe recover in her bedroom, no matter the sneezes. At the workbench in her garage, Nora drafts scalding notes for the parents of the monsters who tortured Babe. Then she stencils the words WATCH FOR DEAF CAT! in red lettering on a dozen posterboard signs. She slams the letters in the appropriate mailboxes and tacks the signs to telephone poles. Her exposed ankles grow wet from the dew upon the thick grass.

III.

Wanda is working the tollbooth when Bister stops. She wears a surgical mask over her mouth and nose because the fumes bother her. Bister doesn't need a mask, but he's thinking of getting one to deter strangers from chatting with him. Wanda doesn't charge Bister, and he drives through to the memorial.

Just past the OceanNation billboard, thick skid marks begin. The dark lines left by the truck's tires nearly reach the ditch. Before exiting his car, Bister tries to imagine what happened. The truck driver slammed on the brakes, clearly. He wonders why. From drivers he knows the truck was hauling lumber. He remembers the driver. She looked angry. He also remembers the unbound chains trailing the truck. A pole came loose and struck the Impala. The lumber is nowhere in sight. Once struck, the Impala must have lost control. There's a carpet of crushed glass, too small to sweep up, collecting sun on the concrete.

The boy in the backseat—the one Bister remembers seeing—somehow withstood the devastating impact.

It's easy to tell where the Impala came to rest. It is where Mindy and three men are huddled next to the scorched earth. Her blue Jetta's hazards flash on the shoulder. Everyone's wearing a shade of black.

Bister takes a deep breath, steps out of his mother's Subaru, and approaches Mindy. "Hey," he says.

It takes Mindy a moment to place Bister.

"Glad you could make it," she says. "I wish you would have brought friends."

Bister shoves his hands into his pockets. "Some people said they'd show."

Mindy's black shirt is dotted with pink flowers. Her long hair is tied back. She is leaning into a shovel. "If they were going to come, they'd have been here by now. That journalist dropped the ball. There wasn't a whisper about this in the *Observer*."

"People don't give a shit," a man holding a large wreath says.

"Some do," Mindy says.

"Plenty do," Bister says.

"Oh yeah," the man says, "and some people know you're supposed to wear black to a funeral."

Bister looks down at his white shirt.

"It's not a funeral," Mindy says. "Just go dig, Dave."

"I'm sorry," Bister says. "I would have worn black if I knew."

"It's fine," Mindy says.

"I have two crosses in my trunk. Do you think we should erect them?"

"Crosses? We've got orange trees."

"A guy offered the crosses. He was pretty insistent."

"Do you know if the victims were Christian?"

"No. I also collected fifty bucks for the little boy."

"Little boy?"

"The kid who survived."

"That would be Veronica."

"A girl?"

"Yeah," Mindy frowns. "Why did you think it was a boy?"

"I saw him."

"You saw *her*. She's been taken to Brunswick General. You can drop the money off there. And find out if she's Christian. If so, I'm cool with the crosses." Mindy turns her attention to Dave, who is digging with fury. "Hey," she shouts, "you're going too deep."

When she walks away, Bister isn't sure if he should follow. He's vaguely aware that this is a moment when his head is filled with cobwebs. The boy was a girl named Veronica. He's got fifty dollars in his pocket and two crosses in his mother's car. And Mindy has walked away.

A passing car honks its horn in support.

Julie, several car-lengths behind the honking vehicle, clutches the steering wheel in her Jeep Wrangler. The old Jeep is what she drives when she's off duty. She quits shouting at the man on the radio and tries to figure out why the person in front of her honked the horn. Then she gets it. A cluster of people have gathered along the side of the road where she murdered that family.

Julie just got out of a meeting with her boss at the lumber transportation services. He decided it was best for her to take some leave time. To help sort things out.

"Sort things out?" Julie said. "People are dead because of me."

"It wasn't your fault," her boss said. "You need to remember that. 'Cause if it was your fault, someone might claim it was also Hefty Haulers fault since you were driving for us at the time of the incident. And we don't want that, right?"

Julie didn't know what she wanted. She didn't want to drive trucks anymore. Her previous job was in lawn maintenance. She worked for the state mowing grass along the sides of I-95. Her crew was in charge of about twenty-five miles. After they cut back the northbound scruff, the southbound needed mowing again. In her first week, Julie plowed over a family of ducks. The bodies were minced unceremoniously. A few feathers hung in the air. When she confided how she felt to her coworkers, they told her it came with the territory. They each had their own animal story to tell, which they did over beers in a Brunswick bar called Dirty Mugs. Julie wasn't cheered by the stories. The next day she tried to mow cautiously. Still, she suspected something slow might linger underfoot. So she decided, after she had mowed the stretch of stuff she was supposed to mow for the day, to climb down from the machine, hoisting a big broom, and spend the evening, her own time, walking through the tall brush and trying to rustle up and frighten whatever lived along the shoulder she was going to mow the next day. Every night she had to pick brambles and twigs from her socks. Then she shredded a nest of baby possums and called it quits.

Now—despite what her boss says—she's responsible for the death of two people from New Hampshire. If she'd been paying better attention and not arguing with the man on the radio...if she had looked out the rearview and seen the trailing chains...if she left the mill one minute later or stayed at the tollbooth longer...if she just swerved to the left…if it'd been a different tree with deeper roots that grew in another forest and was spared the saw…if she'd kept her job in lawn maintenance…if she had double checked those locks—she used to double check them…if only it had been raining; she's more cautious when windshield blades are swishing…if only she'd gone to college…if only she'd stayed on I-95…if only…if only…if only…if only…ifonly…ifonly.

———

Brunswick General is quiet. When Bister visited his mother in the late afternoons, it was quiet, too.

The receptionist at the front desk looks similar to the woman at the front desk of the hospital in Binghamton. Both women are unsmiling.

"Hi," Bister says. "I'm here to see Veronica. The little girl who was in that car accident on the expressway?"

"And you are?"

"Bister."

"Blister?"

"Bister."

The receptionist is named Robin, according to her nametag.

"It's a color. A shade of brown. My mother paints. I guess your mother likes birds."

"Excuse me?"

"Robin. Your name."

Robin frowns. Her eyelids cover most of her eyes. "Are you her brother? A cousin, maybe?"

"I'm an only child. So are my parents. Children, I mean. Only children."

"So you're not related to Ms. Veronica Lattimore?"

"No."

"Then you can't see her."

"It will only take a second. We collected some money."

"I'll make sure she gets it."

Bister sets the cash on the counter. "How is she doing? Will she wake up?"

"She's not asleep. She bumped her head and can't remember anything." Robin thumbs through the cash.

"Will she get better?"

"Not for you or me to say."

"Do you know her faith?"

The receptionist quits counting the bills and glares at Bister. "What kind of question is that?"

"Could I maybe ask her?"

"Son," the receptionist says, "is there something wrong with you? She's not some kind of spectacle. I think you need to leave. I'll be sure her guardian gets this donation."

Bister runs a hand across his face. He sees, down the hall, a drinking fountain and suddenly he has trouble swallowing. "I'm sorry," he says. "I need a drink."

The puce-colored linoleum squeaks under Bister's shoes. When he's at the fountain, he presses the button and drinks deeply. While his head is bent, he observes a gaunt woman in a wheelchair alone and waiting to be taken somewhere. Lowered, he is eye level with her and she is staring with unblinking, yolky eyes. She isn't looking at him, exactly; Bister happens to be standing in her line of vision. She may have been regarding the drinking fountain for several minutes and he simply happened to occupy the space.

When he's done, Bister rises and wipes his mouth with the back of his hand. "Are you thirsty?" he asks.

The woman doesn't reply, but she may have nodded her head in affirmation.

"Here," he says, walking to her side. "I'll push you on over."

She doesn't weigh much. It's easy for him to wheel her to the fountain. When she's close, he presses the button and water cascades in a nice, strong flow.

"There you go," he says, "lean in."

To the best of his knowledge, the woman hasn't blinked. In fact, Bister notices too late, her eyes begin to fill with fear. When she opens her wet mouth, she does not drink. A loud, low moan erupts from her hollow chest and washes over Bister. The pain-laced bellow fills the empty hallway with a terrible and familiar loneliness.

IV.

Bugs hang in the air around the lightbulb in the tollbooth. Crickets hiss. Bister applies more mosquito repellent. All the cars that pass are places he's never been: Tucson, Tahoe, Santa Fe, Cheyenne, Sedona.

A worried woman in a Malibu asks, "Are you guys going to close the road tomorrow?"

"No. Why would we?"

"Arabelle's on her way."

"Who?"

"The hurricane. It's supposed to be a direct hit. Haven't you heard?"

"Maybe," Bister says. The name does sound familiar. He's overheard it mumbled on car radios.

"Be safe," the woman says.

Between cars, Bister takes out his phone. He's planning on checking on the weather when he sees that he has a voicemail message. He never receives messages. Two thoughts pop into his head simultaneously: *Is it from Dad?* and *Why didn't I feel the phone vibrate?*

The message is from Bister's boss, Milt. Milt says they're planning on staying open tomorrow night but stay sharp. He'll call back if things change.

"Why didn't I feel the phone vibrate?"

"Beats me," the old man in the Lexus says. He just kind of materialized. "Turn the ringer on."

"I will."

"How'd those crosses turn out, bub?"

"What?" Bister says. "Oh, right. We didn't use them. They're in my car."

"What do you mean?"

"Well, it's my mom's car. They're in the trunk. I'll grab them."

"I don't want them back!" the man blurts. "You can't return a cross."

"What do you want me to do with them?"

"Put them in the ground, that's what. That's where they belong. Why didn't you use them; weren't they good enough?"

"No. I mean, yes. They're fine. It's just that we don't know if the family was religious."

"You think they were atheists?"

"I don't think they were anything. I'm sorry this didn't work out. It was a nice thought, but I can't do it."

"I got to tell you, I'm disappointed." The man purses his lips and shakes his head. "I thought you were better than this."

Bister bites his tongue and doesn't say, *Who the fuck are you, old man?* Instead, he casts his eyes to the rubbery horizon and says, "One dollar."

"What?"

"The toll." Bister raises the gate.

The man *tsks* when he crumbles the dollar and tosses it at Bister's face. As he speeds away, the wheels squeal.

Kate, the woman driving the powder-blue Volkswagen, witnessed the tense exchange at the booth. "Did you see that?" she asks her husband, Bill. Bill has his phone in his lap and is reading an article about daddy-longlegs.

"No," he mutters.

"That guy in front of us was really rude." Kate pulls forward. To Bister, she asks, "What was that all about?"

Instead of answering, Bister simply shakes his head. "It's a dollar."

"I know it's a dollar," Kate says. "We pass through nearly every night. Don't you remember?"

"Kate," Bill says, "just give him a dollar."

"I'm sorry," Bister says.

"You don't have to be sorry." Kate hands the money over. "It's fine."

"I'll remember you next time."

"That's all right. It's not necessary. I mean, I was just trying to say that I know how much to pay."

"Kate," Bills says, "let's go."

"Right," Bister says. He raises the gate. "Have a nice night."

"*You* have a nice night," Kate insists. "I hope it gets better."

When they are back on the road, Kate says, "Didn't that guy seem really sad to you?"

"Not really," Bill says.

"Every time he's working I've gotten a weird vibe from him, which I haven't been able to pinpoint until now. He's a lost soul."

"A lost soul? Jesus, Kate."

"Yeah. Exactly that. If you paid any attention you'd know what I mean."

Kate and Bill work at the paper mill in Brunswick and commute to Heron Hills. Kate works in sales and gets through the grind of her days believing that somebody might write something important and print it on paper that comes from the mill. Bill is a foreman who works out in the stockyard and is in charge of getting the lumber trucks loaded and secured. He swears he double-checked the locks on the truck involved in the accident. The truth is it's loud in the lumberyard. The air is filled with buzz saws. Bill wears ear plugs and even with them, it's difficult to concentrate.

"Whatever," Bill says. He closes his eyes to rest.

Married at eighteen, Kate and Bill are now nearly forty. They had once been a happily conscientious couple. They both agreed that all parents were selfish and misguided for bringing a child into this cruel world. In their early twenties they built a bonfire on the beach and tossed all of the pictures of their parents and grandparents into it. Bill even tossed in his own baby pictures. At the community college they earned science degrees and protested incinerators, beach erosion, rubber, and the government. In their late twenties, Kate and Bill stared hard at their marriage and decided it was a drag. They experimented with drugs, swapped each other with sexually voracious couples, changed jobs, refurbished the attic, took up jogging, dabbled in a pastiche of religions, cried, fought, turned thirty, went to couples' counseling, separated, debated divorce, flew around the world, planted an evergreen, volunteered at shelters, clung onto each other with vehement desperation, naturally drifted apart, entertained the stock market, and admitted that they had been foolish at eighteen when they thought parents were evil; after all, where would we be without them?

And then, six months ago, on their way home, bored, Kate said, "Bill, I'm bored, give me something to think about."

Bill, who had been thinking about clipping his fingernails, said, whimsically, "Try not thinking of anything."

"Nothing?"

"Zip."

"Zero?"

"Nada."

Kate thought as she drove from Brunswick, past the tollbooth, onto the expressway, past the OceanNation billboard, and nearly to the truck rest stop before she said, "It's the *only* number."

Bill had been dozing while Kate had her epiphany. "There are other numbers," he responded, sitting upright in his seat and shaking his head to stimulate blood in his brain.

"Well," said Kate, absolute in her discovery, "count from zero to one."

"Zero, one," Bill played along.

"What about point zero-one?"

"OK, point zero-one, point zero-two, point zero-three, all the way to one."

"What about point zero-zero-one?"

"Yeah, sure, point zero-zero-one, point zero-zero-zero-zero-zero-one, if you want to get technical. You could keep adding zeroes if you want."

"Exactly," Kate exclaimed, slapping the steering wheel with her palms. "There are an infinite number of possibilities between zero and one. You could never count from zero to one, ever. There's always something in between."

"Mathematicians don't even consider zero a number at all. It's just a circle—a continuum," Bill said, proud of his point. "It's everything."

"No, it's nothing. And if zero's not a number then there's no such thing as numbers at all."

"Does that mean you're not turning forty in a few months?"

"Just hear me out," Kate replied. "Without numbers we don't really have time. And without time we don't have history. If there's no history, there's nothing. Zero!" Kate exclaimed.

"That's not what I had in mind when I told you not to think."

Kate pulled into their driveway full of ideas. She always suspected life was pointless. Now she knew why—there really isn't anything. After a while this revelation led her to depression. For a few months, she sulked. A holiday happened. Birthdays. She was surprised how easily she could convince Bill that everything was fine. *Just fine. I'm fine.* Then, several months ago, over a lukewarm dinner, Kate said she didn't know why they bothered living. "Why don't we kill each other," she'd asked.

Bill toyed with his peas. He was thinking about wearing earplugs all the time. "All right. How do you want to do it?"

"I'm serious, Bill."

"Poison?"

"I want you to explain to me why life is worth living."

"Two nooses? Two stools?"

"You're no help."

"You're right," Bill said. "I'm sorry. What did you have in mind, honey?"

"We need to reconnect with something happy *that has already happened* and use it as a springboard to living a meaningful life *now*," Kate said.

Bill didn't know what his wife was talking about, really, but it was easier to acquiesce.

Kate devised a plan: without revealing it to the other, they each began a personal project. First, they needed their personal space. Kate claimed the attic, Bill settled for the tool shed. These spaces were private. The projects were for themselves. "We work alone so we can be better *together*," Kate said.

Now, back at home with the car's engine cooling in the garage, Kate excuses herself to climb the stairs to the attic. She slips the key into the lock on the short door and ducks to enter. Inside is a little light from the shuttered window, musty boxes, an old loom, and a ten-pound bag of powdered concrete.

When she first climbed into the attic, Kate poked around the boxes for inspiration. They were mostly filled with holiday trinkets, old bed linen and dishes. In one box, though, she found books— Bill's textbooks from college. He had taken a required English survey course. Kate received college credit from high school and wasn't forced to take English at the community college. Seeing his books annoyed her. Between them, she was the one more likely to read. When she was a girl, Kate remembered, she used to rifle through mysteries at her grandmother's house in the late summers before middle school started. Grandma left Kate alone with the books and didn't ask anything in return. For giving her independence, Kate loved her grandmother. In the books, she lazily drifted away. She daydreamed of other places and had whole conversations with characters—gave advice to the detectives and tried to coax admissions out of the suspects. Most of the time she could guess who did it halfway through.

Grandma spent her time quilting.

"Didn't Grandma once say, 'Quilts tell stories'?" Kate asked herself, aloud. "She might not have said that exactly. Probably she didn't."

But Grandma made them, good and strong with flowers and butterflies and balloons.

It took Kate a month to quilt the basics of a blanket, stopping as she did to thumb through Bill's old American poetry anthology. The poems she liked best made her sad. Emily Dickinson, Robert Frost, and Wallace Stevens. She memorized a few dreamy lines by Carl Sandburg because she liked hearing her voice say—"I remember lean ones among you/Throats in the clutch of hope/Lips written over with strivings/Mouths that kiss only for love."

She kept at the quilting. Her hands slowly became deft. She dug deeper into Bill's box and found *David Copperfield*. She read, "I had thought, much and often, of my Dora's shadowing out to me what might have happened, in those years that were destined not to try us; I had considered how the things that never happen, are often as much realities to us, in their effects, as those that are accomplished." This passage triggered a memory of her first love, Ryan; he'd been in the high school production of *A Midsummer Night's Dream*.

She read a used copy of *Madame Bovary* which she thought was so-so. Kate was more taken by the inscription on the first page. It wasn't written to Bill. It read: *Dominique, read deeply. Love deeply. Pass it on*. There was a smudged date and an illegible signature beneath the thick "USED" stamp.

Kate wondered aloud, "What does the inscriber mean by *it*? Pass the love? Pass the book? *It* has been collecting dust up here all these years. Fitting."

By the time the blanket was ready for a pattern, Kate was midway through *The Bell Jar* and having snippets of pensive conversation with Esther Greenwood.

The quilt sat on her lap, uninspired.

"What is the point, Grandma?" she asked.

Without thinking too much about it, she stitched an enormous O into her blanket. When the O was double stitched, she stitched it again.

"If quilting tells a story, Grandma, I'd like to know how it ends. Esther knew, didn't she?"

At the bottom of Bill's box was a collection of Shakespeare's tragedies.

Kate started stitching an S on both sides of the O—SOS. Not that she expected anyone to rescue her.

For his wife's sake, Bill tried, too. He sat on a fold-out chair beneath a flickering light in the tool shed for a week thinking it through. When a spider crossed in front of him on its way from one shadow to the next, Bill remembered days as a boy playing with daddy-longlegs in the woods. He used to yank the legs off the spiders. He'd been told that they grew back. Also, in the woods, the time his brother pushed him from a tree and gave him a concussion. And poison ivy, ant bites, ghosts on the wind in the leaves, the well, an abandoned cabin with broken-out windows, his first kiss, hide and seek, the two weeks it took him to chop down a twenty-foot maple with his father's ax just to watch it fall and yell, with everything in him, "Timber!"

Those woods, Bill thought, *those woods*.

Bill's father would later sell the property so that it could be farmed for its trees. The Brunswick Paper Mill bought it up. This gave Bill an in with the company that he fought for years and years not to take.

The spider moved into the corner. Spiders were certainly a part of his youth. *Why not farm daddy-longlegs?* Bill thought. It made as much sense as anything else. It was easy to find a dozen of the spiders behind the shed, in the gutters, near the neighbor's peonies. He plucked them by a leg and dropped them into a cracked twenty-gallon aquarium with a netted top. He fed them flies and moths. Then, there they were, a dozen trapped spiders spinning webs. Bill watched them for hours. He wanted more. He wanted them to have baby spiders, a whole group of them. A cluster, he learned from a quick online search, is what you call a bunch of spiders. And daddy-longlegs could hatch hundreds of eggs in a batch. In a *clutch*.

Playing the odds, Bill put two spiders in six Mason jars. He labeled the jars, .01, .001, .0001, .00001, .000001, and .0000001.

For two weeks, Bill waited and tapped his foot on the concrete floor of the shed. Sometimes the neighborhood cat—the one with bluish-colored fur—wandered over and spied on him. He didn't like that cat. It always seemed to be watching him, judging. Kate used to want a cat but Bill did not. When he was a kid, a boy named Tommy demonstrated how you could tie firecrackers into a loop so that when you lit it, there would be a chain reaction. Last year, the Fourth of July was rained out. The fireworks he bought for the event were in a box on a shelf in the shed above a wheelbarrow.

"Right there," he said to the cat, pointing.

Bill's project was spiders, not cats. Sometimes he had trouble focusing. His mind wandered into dead ends that always left him somewhat surprised.

To keep himself on track, Bill researched daddy-longlegs. Apparently, they could kill black widows. And there was a rumor that the spiders themselves were venomous, only their fangs were too small to penetrate human flesh. Arachnologists claimed this was a myth.

Sitting alone in the damp shed, Bill grabbed a fat spider and let it crawl along his arm. He wondered what it would taste like. "If they're not venomous, are they at least poisonous?" He never knew anyone, when he was young, brave enough to eat one. Not even Tommy. And hey, suddenly he was kind of thinking about his childhood. And that was his wife's charge, right? Dredge up something good from *then* in order to be happy *now*.

What else was there other than the woods, spiders, and that bully Tommy? All the photographs he had from his childhood—school shots and family gatherings—had been tossed into the fire. All he had now were memories, and, quite suddenly, he recalled his dad punching him in the mouth for swearing. Afterward, Bill fled to the safety of the trees and stayed there overnight.

But this was not a happy thought. His wife had said *happy.*

The same night that Kate started talking to Ophelia up in the attic and decided to fill her quilt with powdered concrete and stitch it extra-strong, the spiders in Mason jar .001 produced eggs. Bill thought the eggs looked like a spoonful of cottage cheese.

A deadly spoonful?

An idea hatched in the dead end of Bill's mind.

Now, after Kate has withdrawn her lips into a toothy smile and ascended the narrow steps to the attic, Bill waits for her footfalls to fade. He opens a can of tuna and dumps the food into a metal bowl. Grabbing a spoon, he hustles out to the shed. Very carefully, with his excited hands shaking, he scoops the spider eggs from the Mason jar and mixes them into the tuna. Then, before retiring to the safety of the tool shed, he sets the bowl in a patch of moonlight in the overgrown lawn and says, "Here, kitty, kitty, kitty."

V.

Wearing a mask helps. Bister bought one before his shift. Although it's difficult to breathe and people look at him funny, he has found that he simply has to grunt or mutter when anyone says something to him and they leave him alone. People have been talking nonstop about Arabelle: *We're right in the storm's path* and *It might be a Cat. 3 by tonight* and *I'm going to board up our windows but our neighbor isn't* and *I've seen plenty worse than this one. Just gonna ride it out.*

"Can you believe that the Q-Mart downtown is charging eight dollars for a case of water?" a woman in an Odyssey asks. "That's unconscionable."

Bister gives a quick nod, mutters something the woman can't hear, and raises the gate.

Behind her is Mindy. Bister's heart does a quick cartwheel. When she's next to him and he smells the coconut, he says, "I went and visited Veronica."

"What?" Mindy asks. "Why are you wearing that? Do you have a cold?"

"No," Bister says. He pulls the mask down. "It's a buffer for chit-chat. Not meant for you. I mean, I don't mind talking to you. I look forward to it, actually. Anyway, I went to the hospital but I don't know if the little girl is Christian."

"Yeah," Mindy says, "I don't think it's the mask. You just kind of talk weird. It's hard to follow what you're saying."

"Oh," Bister says. "Sorry about that."

"No need to apologize. Here." Mindy hands Bister a twenty. "There's a storm coming. Let the next nineteen people pass on me."

Bister slides the mask back over his mouth and nose. "I like you," he says. "Your kindness is rare. I want to buy you a cup of coffee."

Mindy flashes her half smile. "Stay safe, all right?"

Bister raises the gate. He keeps it open and waves cars through. A Shadow passes. A Mirage, a Soul, a Vibe, a Spirit, an Echo. The old man in the Lexus stops even though the gate is open.

"Hey," the man says. "I want to apologize about my behavior yesterday. I shouldn't have lost my cool."

"It's free. Move on," Bister shouts through his mask. "It's free. Move on. It's free. Move on. It's free. Move on."

"All right," the man says, raising his arms in defense. "I'm going."

Larry, in the tan pickup truck, is the twentieth car behind Mindy and he's forced to stop.

"Why can't I go through?" he asks.

The worker says something, Larry thinks. "Never mind," he says. He pays his dollar and drives ahead, trying to stay focused. Tonight he can't be distracted.

Larry has never seen any herons in the Heron Hills Lakeview development. He's seen plenty of ducks and geese in the small, fountain-festooned pond. The HHL homeowners association is in the process of having a gate installed, but it isn't operational yet.

Larry works for a computer software company in Brunswick and has difficulty impressing his coworkers and peers due to his inability to say the right thing appropriately. He has no timing. Today, in the elevator with Sam, Larry said, "I wonder if Arabelle will hit…" just as Sam said, "So, Lar, what's the highest category storm you've been in?" Larry replied, "Four years ago when…" as Sam responded, "The meteorologists say…" When the elevator stopped, Sam stepped out, and Larry said, "I'd prefer to be called Larry…" while Sam emphatically said, "See you around."

In his studio apartment, with his computer, Larry is a different man. He belongs to an underground online club who call themselves the Preying Mantids. The credo of the Mantids is: *If you're not pulling the prank, the prank's on you.*

It took Larry some time to think through a prank to be proud of, something to claim for his own, to be remembered by. The idea came while visiting his parents in suburban Atlanta. He arrived early on a Sunday, the parents were at the mall and the key was under the mat, so he let himself in. The act, Larry realized, was gold.

Starting in working-class neighborhoods, Larry made his way, in the dark and wearing a fly mask, from doormat to doormat taking a key from one house and replacing it with a key from someone else's house. The victims were both locked out of their own homes and given access to their neighbor's. The Preying Mantids were full of online praise. In order to raise the stakes, Larry has decided to prank the snobs in Heron Hills Lakeview. Even rich people leave a spare key under the mat, he bets. With the hurricane on the way, many residents—with their second homes—have abandoned the neighborhood. The wind and the rain should blur the doorbell cameras. It could be an epic night.

Now, sitting in his car next to the tennis courts, Larry slides the fly mask over his face and awaits darkness.

Arabelle arrives. She swallows the remnants of sun. Rain and wind crash against the Heron Hills pier upon which Kate stands. She's wrapped up in her quilt and staring blankly at the hypnotic and phosphorescent wave chop. Kate can feel the powdered concrete she carefully stitched into the patchwork as it begins to harden in the rain. All she has to do is jump into the turbulent water and sink. Below the surface is calm. Beneath the water is peace.

The note she left on the kitchen counter before driving to the pier reads, *I realize that happiness is not possible and I am not unhappy about this.* She's sure that this will baffle her husband.

"The end," she says to the wind, cinching the quilt tightly around her and dropping into the choppy water. She bobs and waits for the concrete to harden. When it does, she sinks. Just when she's certain she's on her way to oblivion, the quilt rips. The concrete is too strong. She should have offered more stitches. Her fingers cannot grip the block of concrete and, with a fistful of fabric, she buoys to the surface. The waves—at Arabelle's command—pitch her to shore.

Inland, Nora finally finds the strength to thrust the shovel into the soft ground. Her cat Babe is dead. This morning she found him frothing and sick in the garden. She raced to the vet in Brunswick. Apparently the cat ate something very bad. Maybe a poisonous toad?

"Perhaps," the vet suggested, "it'd be best if we put him down gently."

Nora lightly petted the scorched fur around Babe's neck. She blinked through tears to stare into the cat's sick yellow eyes. "I'm sorry," she said to her deaf cat. "Please forgive me." Then she sneezed.

Now, by the peonies in her backyard, where Babe used to lounge in the sun, Nora digs. Out of the corner of her eye she spots her sketchy neighbor Bill hurrying over with a green-speckled umbrella. Nora has wondered what Bill does all night in the shed that divides their side-yard property. Sometimes he's in there well after midnight.

When Bill gets close he says, "Have you seen my wife around?"

Nora wipes her nose on her sleeve. Rain makes sound bouncing off the umbrella. "No. I've been out."

"She left a strange note. I'm sure it's nothing. Hey," Bill says, "what's in the box?"

"Babe. I had to put him down."

"Who's Babe?"

"My cat. He ate something bad. The vet thinks it was a *Rhinella marina*, whatever that is."

"That was *your* cat?"

"Yeah. He was the greatest. I got him from the shelter when he was just a kitten. He was the smallest of the litter. His coat was so soft. The veterinarian said he'd never seen fur that was quite that color."

Bill's thoughts drift while Nora reminisces. *So,* he thinks, *those daddy longlegs are poisonous. Who knew? I wonder how many clutches it would take to kill a human...*

Lightning strikes so close the thunder shakes bones.

"I better hurry," Nora says. "It's probably not wise to be out here."

"True," Bill says, backing up. "Say, I'd like to have you over for dinner soon. You can finish what you were saying about Babe. Kate likes cats."

Up the expressway, the young orange trees Mindy planted along the side of the road uproot and scatter. The OceanNation billboard shakes vehemently.

Julie's Jeep is in the median. With a bucket of bleach by her side, she furiously scrubs the concrete, trying to remove the skid marks. In the darkness, with the blinding rain, an oncoming car would only have a split second to swerve to the left—the way she didn't steer the rig—before pulverizing her. But she doesn't care, doesn't care, doesn't care. Just scrubs, scrubs, scrubs. The skin on her knuckles scrapes against the road. Her blood mixes with the bleach and the rain and the impossibly thick rubber stains. Early today she'd spoken with her father. She told him about the accident, the *manslaughter*. Told him she was going to quit. Told him she hadn't slept in a real long time.

Dad said it'd pass. Said all things do. "It's not the passing that counts, it's the doing. You have an opportunity to reassess your life. Do a little soul-searching. Figure out who you are. Who are you, Jewels?"

"I don't know," Julie said then. It seemed like a trick question.

Now, though, after an afternoon at Dirty Mugs, she's got an answer. Lots of answers. So many. She is plenty of people all in one nobody. Or nobody all in one plenty of people. "I'm a little teapot," she tells the wind. "I'm fee-fie-foe-fum. A handful of magic beans. The bucket of water Jack couldn't fetch. Humpty tipping off the wall. I'm the fall. I am a stain. Wood grain. The residue of disappointment scratched from a worthless lottery ticket. I am the instant before the pounce. I'm the cat, I'm the mouse. I swerve too soon. I'm Quasimodo's only friend. I am the last piece of dirt to settle on the grave. I am the blade before it's unsheathed. Grass covering a rattler. I'm the piper's fife. The rook's tune. The hobo's bed. I'm the itsy-bitsy fucking spider's web. I am the gulp between sober and drunk."

When she sees headlights bearing down, Julie sets the scrub brush aside. From her knees she lifts her head to the clouds. "I promise," she says, "that if this car spares me, tomorrow I'll do better."

The wind and rain that Arabelle scuttles across the Brunswick Expressway has come all the way from Africa. It crashes into the tollbooth with tremendous force. Bister stands with his feet apart and contemplates sprinting to the Subaru where it's safer.

Everything inside the booth is alive: the cash register jangles and the windows shake. There's a ringing in Bister's ears that he discovers is actually coming from the cellphone in his pocket. He'd forgotten that he'd turned it on. Thinking that it's Milt calling to tell him to shut the road down, Bister fetches it. When he checks the number, he immediately recognizes it.

"Dad?" he says.

"Hello?" the father asks. "Is that you?"

Bister swipes the mask from his face. "It's me," he shouts. "I'm in a hurricane. You called. I'm so glad. Mom's back?"

"Bister? I can't hear you so good."

"Dad, it's me. Is Mom awake?"

"I'm not sure if you can hear me. I'm calling to tell you."

"I can hear you. Where's Mom? Can you put her on?"

"No. I can't. She's gone, son. She let go."

"What?"

"Gone."

A great, merciful gust of wind rips the tollbooth from the earth. Inside, Bister feels himself soar into the bewildering sky. In his mind, the booth smashes to the concrete road and shatters into a million pieces.

VI.

Veronica remembers.

The little girl had been bouncing on a trampoline and now she is not. Her body comes to rest on the taut, synthetic rubber netting. Someone downwind is burning leaves and this smell—thick as syrup—is not unlike the scent produced from the paper mill in southern Georgia. The odor triggers the memories. They spill out as she lies on her back and faces the partly cloudy afternoon New Hampshire sky.

She remembers chewing gum. Trying to blow bubbles, something her best friend Peri does spectacularly.

She remembers her mother's silhouette. Mom sat in the passenger seat doing a crossword puzzle. She was struggling with a five-letter word that started with the letter G. The clue: *A kind of sadness.*

Outside, the grass seemed primitive and dangerous. The tall pine trees were right out of a Dr. Seuss book. If there were clouds, she couldn't see them.

On the radio, she remembers the meteorologist forecasting. She had such a funny accent. Her vowels were drawn out. Sounded like she was trying to speak and chew a mouthful of oatmeal at the same time. *We're gonna have three H's today, folks*, the woman had said. *Heat, haze, and humidity.*

Her dad stopped and paid the toll. She met the eyes of the toll-booth worker. She remembers how peculiar he made her feel. He seemed familiar in a way impossible to pinpoint. He kind of looked the way she thought she'd look if she was a boy and grew up in the South. When he'd said "Hi," she stayed quiet.

Veronica remembers picking at a hangnail on her ring finger.

She remembers keeping track of the colors of passing cars: *blue, dark green, yellow, silver, tan...*

She remembers the pinch of the seatbelt.

She remembers the time—7:47, like the airplane—glowing red on the dash. She'd eaten chicken nuggets with honey mustard dipping sauce for dinner an hour earlier. She dismissed the sudden tightness in her chest as indigestion rather than what it was: a premonition, a warning that she was two minutes away from the end of everything.

She remembers the discarded OceanNation brochures strewn in the seat next to her. Oh, how she'd begged and pleaded with her parents for the vacation. Dad had worked overtime so they could afford it.

She remembers the high-pitched whistle of tires, a short cry from her mother, and the mist of blood on her eyelashes.

She does not remember spinning.

Veronica doesn't know why this happened to her. Why her? Why Mom and Dad? She has no access to the *reason*. She's not familiar with chain reaction. She doesn't quite understand the consequences of an apple core.

Veronica never met Mindy Unger. She might have seen her if the world glowed a shade brighter. Mindy, in her blue Jetta, plays Tammy the Turtle at OceanNation. She sings, "We all live together in the sea!"

On the evening of June 4, Mindy rolled her window down and tossed the remains of an apple she'd finished into the scruff along the Brunswick Expressway—just past the billboard. Veronica couldn't know that a rabid raccoon was pacing the shoulder of the toll road, its head garbled raw. The animal spied the apple, snatched it, and darted into the road.

Veronica has no way of knowing that the raccoon would not be crushed beneath the tires of the yellow Neon, driven by Nora Cavanaugh, who spotted it in the nick of time. She slammed on her brakes and came to a halt.

Veronica will receive anonymous cashier's checks in the mail every other month for many years. Sometimes it's fifty dollars, sometimes it's less. Veronica does not know that Julie Fairmont is the name behind the money. Julie did not get crushed by oncoming traffic the night the hurricane blew through. The car narrowly missed her. It clipped the bucket of bleach, which careened into the ditch. Julie picked herself up.

Julie will try very hard to forgive herself.

Bill Tucker, who is, perhaps, more to blame for the accident than anyone, neglected to click the locks shut. Nobody will ever confront him with this truth. The lies in his life will gather around his ankles and drag him down.

Veronica does not know that the pine pole popped against the expressway at an angle which sent it soaring over Larry Drucker's tan-colored pickup truck. Larry will not appreciate his good fortune. He will soon forget about the accident altogether. His attention will be tied to the computer and to chat rooms and his online pals. Soon,

Larry will get promoted and be able to work from home as a computer programmer. He will go months at a time without leaving his apartment. He will grow. He will ask his heart to work overtime. For the most part, it will.

The slash pine pole, at twenty-three years old, will be shorn into sizeable strips and produced into paper upon which Bister Hale will write a story about his mother.

Veronica has no clue what kinds of fireworks were popping in the mind of the tollbooth worker. She doesn't know that, on his way home for his mother's funeral, Bister passed two sets of crosses along the side of I-95 before he finally pulled into the median next to the third one. Where he stopped was a single cross. It used to be painted white. The wood showed through in strips. The leather strap that bound the sticks was cracked. A name was once painted in gold along the spine but the only remaining letters were *or*. The person who died could have been Victor or Connor or Trevor or Salvador or Junior. *Or*, Bister thought, *just or*. The death of *or*. No more wondering if Mom comes out of the coma or if she does not. He fetched the crosses from the trunk and planted them next to or.

Veronica doesn't know that Bister will revive his mother's garden. In April, so many cucumbers will grow that he's able to share them with his neighbors. His father, someday in the near future, will eat a handful of cherry tomatoes Bister harvested.

When she is older, Veronica will contemplate visiting the scene of the accident. Ultimately, she'll decide not to make the drive down south and she will not learn that the Brunswick Expressway is gone. The road will sink into the swamp. No amount of concrete will keep it unburied.

There are an infinite number of things Veronica does not know. Someday, she won't let this bother her so much.

For now, Veronica is a lonely twelve-year-old girl being drenched by the particulars of her traumatic memory. Tears trickle down her cheeks but they don't stay there. The moisture on her face rises. It lifts higher and higher. Her sorrow forms storm clouds. Her heart is a hurricane.